Utterly Bugged

Ken Tennessen

Illustrations by Kika Esteves

Red Dragonfly Press
Northfield, Minnesota
2013

This is a work of fiction. All characters and events portrayed in this book are either fictitious or used fictitiously.

ISBN 978-1-937693-31-2

ISBN 978-1-937693-32-9 (e-book)

Library of Congress Control Number: 2013932998

Several people read early drafts of several chapters and encouraged me to continue weaving this story. Many thanks to my wife Sandi and my sons Jeff and Greg for support and encouragement. Thanks also to Margi Chriscinske, Rosser and Jo Garrison, Pat Hudson, Bill Oldland, and Steve Valley for advice and helpful suggestions.

I thank Freya Manfred for her thoughtful review and for providing numerous helpful suggestions which greatly improved the manuscript.

One other individual I want to recognize is my cat Lily who accompanied me along the tangled trails of research for this book.

Printed in the United States of America
on 30% recycled stock
by BookMobile, a 100% wind-powered company

Designed and Typeset by Scott King using Menhart MT Std
and Manuscript MT Std for titling. Both digital faces
based upon designs by Czech type designer Oldřich Menhart

Published by Red Dragonfly Press
press-in-residence at the Anderson Center
P. O. Box 406
Red Wing, MN 55066

www.reddragonflypress.org

Contents

Forward

Chapter One: Doctor Snakedoctor 13

Chapter Two: The Stance of the Ants 35

Chapter Three: The Wasp Sting 45

Chapter Four: The Great Mosquito Festival 61

Chapter Five: Fireflies in the Great Lakes 75

Chapter Six: Caterpillars in the Big Apple 91

Chapter Seven: Holy Mantis 113

Chapter Eight: Escape to Chinchipino 131

Chapter Nine: Butterfly High 153

Chapter Ten: Delirium Insectorum 169

Dedicated to all old entomologists
who have been bitten and bugged

Forward

This saga is based on the ramblings of an old entomologist, Dr. Amos P. Garruty, known to his colleagues as "Pancake." I remember well that day I was out roving when this wiry, slender man with gray-black stubble found and detained me. It was the longest, most arduous day of my life, not to mention that I most certainly missed out on several mating opportunities, and in case you don't know, those are precious to us bugs. But, besides his fingers, there was something about him and his anecdotes that captivated me.

I have recorded his story the best I could. The stained, wrinkled notebooks he left behind helped a lot. One thing troubles me. I know there are factual tidbits about us bugs in Garruty's notes, but it seems to me some of his observations and experiences are misguided at best, perhaps even bordering on dementia. And who would know better than me?

Squelchy, the Rove Beetle
Clifton, Tennessee
Fall 2002

Utterly Bugged

I

Doctor Snakedoctor

The slap to his face was so sharp it snapped Garruty out of a stupor and left a warm, rosy welt on his left cheek. He was on a trail in a remote area of the Ozark Mountains and was so deep in thought that he had become oblivious to the pesky deer flies. A piercing bite right on his face by a sneaky one got his attention. *How the hell can they land on your skin and you can't feel'em?* he wondered. It was midmorning on a partly cloudy day in late May, and he was looking for the habitat of two rare dragonflies. He hoped finding these elusive species would help put the final pieces of the puzzle in place for his new hypothesis on insect distributions. *Still, I feel like something's missing,* he continued thinking. *Maybe something in the long-lost past is the key. Something ancient insects went through.*

Garruty retrieved his old Boston Red Sox baseball cap from a side pocket of his backpack and yanked it down on his head as far as it would go.

"The brim of this old cap will keep'em off my face at least," he muttered.

Amos Garruty was in his element. The opportunity to go on extended field trips was the reason he had retired early at age 58. His 32-year career as an entomologist for the federal government never allowed him enough time to pursue his own field studies on insects. The short vacations he was able to take while working were never enough to satisfy him. Now he could take his time. *After all,* he thought, *I've got a lot of good years left.*

Despite the biting flies swirling around his head, he continued struggling up the narrow, rocky path of a steep ridge. His breathing was getting heavy, even though he was in pretty good shape. Near the top of the ridge he froze. His eyes locked onto a large cylindrical object partly concealed by bushes and tall weeds. He was staring at a large wooden barrel, tipped over on its side. It was nearly four feet across at the ends and wider at the middle. Having never seen a wooden drum such as this, he set his backpack on the ground so he could take a close look. The gray, weathered slats covered here and there with lichen and moss told him one thing—this was a very old barrel that had been here a very long time. *It has to be made of oak or hickory, no other wood would last out here.*

Garruty put his insect net down and picked up a stick to clear away the spider webs intertwined with vines of poison ivy at the open end. As he peered into the dim, roomy interior, he could see what looked like an inscription and several unusual drawings close to the middle. His mind raced. *I wonder what kind of spirits this old barrel once held.* He paused, then curiosity got the best of him and he slowly crawled inside to get a better look at the strange writing. He was nearly six feet tall but weighed only 170 pounds, so he was able to fit quite easily.

Once inside, the etchings looked like a language he had not seen before. Even with the poor lighting, he saw that they were more like symbols than any writing. There were ovals with squiggly lines angling inside and jagged lines projecting, like lightning bolts, but they looked as if wood-boring beetles had carved them. And there were several sketches.

He started talking out loud as if recording his observations. "Could be Native American. But these drawings look like some strange prehistoric insects. Geez, look at the triangular spines on the grotesque rectangular head, and there are three pairs of wings!"

He decided to take a picture, figuring maybe later he could find out what it meant. "Good thing I brought my flash," he said under his breath. Finding it difficult to see through the lens, he focused as best he could and pressed the shutter release button; the brief flash was startling in the dim interior. He tried to focus again when suddenly it felt as though the barrel shuddered and moved a bit. Feeling a bit uneasy, he looked out the end, thinking maybe he better get out. But it was too late—before he could move, the huge drum started to roll down the steep hill. He braced himself by forcing his hands and feet against the inside, hoping for the best. Bright colored lights flashed through the interior, so intense he closed his eyes. The back of his head hit the side of the barrel as it flumped down the hill. He was getting nauseous.

Abruptly, the huge drum stopped, rocking and rolling a bit. He was shaking, but not feeling any great pain, and with all limbs functional, he leaned over to the edge of the barrel and crawled out. He tried to stand but lost his balance and caught himself against a tree. Holding onto the trunk to keep his balance, he suddenly felt several sharp, hot stings on his left arm and wrist. Large orange ants were ripping into his flesh like the Azteca ants he'd had a brush with in the tropics! He quickly scraped these marauders off and looked around.

The tree he had grabbed looked like a Cecropia, based on the few large, dissected leaves on its crown. He looked around and saw lush vegetation everywhere, including many types of bromeliads.

"What are these tropical plants doing in Arkansas!?" he exclaimed.

Then he heard a loud hollow call, something like that of an oropendola, a loud black and yellow tropical bird. A large, green and black moth flapped in a zigzag route past him. As sweat beads formed on his face, he began to think that he wasn't in Arkansas anymore. Incredible as it seemed, he must have been transported to some tropical land. *How could this be? And just where am I?*

Garruty's first inclination was to find someone and get help. He found a small path and slipped and slithered downhill, spending as much time on his buttocks as on his feet, hoping it would lead to a house or village. The knot on the back of his head was getting bigger, and he couldn't stop that "Roll out the barrel, we'll have a barrel of fun" tune from ringing in his ears, playing itself over and over, stoking his headache.

While rubbing his temples, he noticed that the path paralleled a small stream, and just ahead there were several small clearings in the forest. Flying about these openings were dragonflies of all sizes and colors; he had never seen such numbers and diversity! Trembling from his ride, but with camera still in hand, he decided to take advantage of this opportunity and started to sneak up on a large, shiny green and red individual perched on the underside of a large tree fern. As he slowly approached, he almost stepped on a snake. The red, yellow and black banding indicated it was either some kind of coral snake or a mimic of one, but he certainly was no expert on tropical snakes.

Garruty stopped. *Slow and steady, don't get too close, just maybe I can photograph this guy.* But the serpent wasn't moving; he wasn't sure if it was even breathing. He snapped a few pictures and then backed up a couple steps, staying close by to see if the snake was actually injured or was just faking death.

After a few minutes the snake still didn't move. Sure looks dead, he thought. He took a small stick and pushed it underneath the middle of the snake, lifting it gently; it squirmed once.

Garruty was about to give up on it when a large dragonfly flew over, circled back, and perched near the snake's head. It was a primitive-looking thing, with stripes of light brown and radiant magenta on its side and a pattern of black rings and pale green diamond-shaped spots on its tail. Garruty noticed that its color pattern resembled that of certain kinds of snakes and there were large leaf-like appendages at the tip of its tail. After a few seconds it flew up and hovered over the motionless snake. The dragonfly maneuvered up and down for a short time, after which it flew in small figure 8s over the entire length of the snake's long rigid body. It landed on the snake's tail, rubbed it eyes with its forelegs, after which it made short hopping flights up toward the snake's head. With each hop, the dragonfly tapped the tip of its tail to the snake's skin. When it reached the snake's head, it stuck the tip of its tail into the snake's mouth as if injecting something, then flew upward and repeatedly crashed into the snake right between its eyes! After about seven or eight bombardments of the snake's skull, it teetered upward and pocked Garruty right between the eyes. It then fell to earth, limp and spent.

Somewhat dazed, Garruty rubbed his forehead and out of the corner of his eye caught sight of the snake. It lifted its head, shimmied, and then crawled into the low vegetation.

Appalled, Garruty looked over at the dragonfly—it was lying on its back on the damp clay. He reached down to touch its upwardly extended legs and it latched onto the tip of his finger. He held the stocky insect up and blew a few soft breaths into its face. Its huge greenish-blue, multi-faceted eyes were spellbinding, and he recalled the marvelous dance it had just performed. In an instant it righted itself, whirred its wings and then careened off toward the small stream, disappearing into the lush forest.

Only then did he realize he hadn't taken a single picture of what just happened and he regretted even more his decision not to bring a video camera on his trip. Disappointed with himself, he continued down the crooked, slippery little path. *Guess I better find out where I am and get some help. It sure looks like the Neotropics. If that's right, how the hell did I get here, and how will I get back to the U.S.A.?* he puzzled as if someone was with him. Then a scientific realization struck. That dragonfly was a Petaltail! Now this was very unusual, as he knew that only one species of Petaltail occurred in the Neotropics, and that species was smaller and very differently colored than the one he'd just seen. Moreover, that species lived in a cooler, high-elevation climate, not in the humid rainforest.

What is going on? Could I have stumbled onto a new species? And did that strange Petaltail actually revive that snake? he wondered. *Maybe they are snakedoctors*, he thought. He had always scoffed at the old wife's tales about how dragonflies healed snakes, stung horses and sewed up boys' ears who lied. *Snakedoctors really curing snakes? How will I ever uncork this 'insanity' to the scientific community without definite proof, without getting laughed at?* he wondered.

Then something else occurred to him, something that gave him a definite case of the willies. Animals had been using the path he was on, not humans. There were different kinds of triangular depressions and claw marks in the wet clay, nothing like the rounded depressions bare human feet or flat marks that shoes would make.

Senses alert, he trekked along the path for about half an hour, noticing that the sky was becoming cloudier. Drenched with sweat and with his headache getting worse, he reached a lowland area where there were several shallow vegetated wetlands and open ponds. Snakedoctors were teeming here; suddenly he was a biologist again. But despite his past experience with these insects in the tropics, he recognized few of the species. Although still befuddled about where he was, the thought of seeing new snakedoctors and perhaps another rendezvous with an injured snake overcame his quest for help, and he started searching in earnest.

After awhile, he noticed a flurry of activity at the edge of a small wet-season pool. There, lying motionless at the edge of the shallow water, was a baby snake. At least a dozen bright red snakedoctors were grasping it with their long legs and struggling to fly. Slowly the snakedoctors partly dragged, partly lifted the little snake out of the water and onto a little sunlit sandy spot. It had a gash on its neck and was limp. Several of the snakedoctors tended to the wound while the others landed on the snake and repeatedly fanned its body with their long, yellow wings. He slowly closed in, focused and took a picture, but the flash spooked them and they quickly disappeared. *That's odd,* he thought, *the light usually doesn't bother them. Darn, if I hadn't left my net and backpack behind, I could have collected one of them.* Then he saw the little snake begin to move; it appeared to be recuperating so Garruty picked it up and gently placed it in some vegetation where it quickly disappeared. Excited about what he'd already seen, Garruty spent a couple more hours in this area, seeing some strange insects but no more ailing snakes.

During Garruty's narrow-minded effort to discover more about the snakedoctors, he had been unaware of how cloudy it had gotten. The ever-darkening sky was bearing down on his very being. The ant bites on his arm were itching and burning. He hurried further along the path, but it gradually narrowed, becoming more overgrown.

After a few hundred yards, the path ended near an enormous, buttressed kapok tree. Around the tree lay only wilderness. The jungle was quiet, and he figured the snakedoctors must have disappeared in the heavy jungle.

He uttered aloud, "I better follow their lead and take shelter from the pending deluge."

Now late in the day, he still hadn't found any sign of human activity. His dry tongue and cotton throat reminded him he had not taken his canteen with him when he crawled into the giant oak drum. All he had was an empty plastic bottle in the side pocket of his cargo pants. He turned to find another path, thinking it seemed like ages since he crawled into that strange vessel back in Arkansas, and his mind drifted back to his home in Alabama. There was no one there to miss him, just his little cat. His ex-wife Adele had left him years ago, though he couldn't remember how long it had been. All of a sudden he felt lonely and empty, and a chill crept over his damp skin.

"Better find shelter, idiota," he muttered.

He retraced his steps for a ways and at the edge of a small clearing found several large plants that looked a lot like elephant's-ear or *Gunnera* with leaves several feet across. With his small pocketknife, he cut off several of the large, stout leaves and pieced them together, overlapping them until he had a mat large enough to cover himself. He bent several slender saplings down to the ground and fastened the "leaf roof" over the top. He also laid a few of the leaves underneath the shelter on which to sit. He then made a funnel out of a smaller, shiny-clean leaf to collect rainwater in the empty plastic bottle.

By this time it was nearly dark, and he felt worn out and hungry; he hadn't seen any fruit trees, or anything else that might be edible. He sat down on the large leaves, trying to relax while waiting for the rain to fall. The combined smells of damp decaying vegetation and fungi filled his nostrils. He hoped his shelter didn't leak too badly. Just before dark, the rain started and shortly the plastic bottle was half full. The water tasted slightly tart, but refreshing, and he drank it down and set it back out under the funnel to collect more. His shelter kept most of the water away, but Garruty's mind was still racing and he knew he was too nervous to fall asleep. As darkness engulfed him, he felt somewhat comforted that he had spent time in the tropics before. His thoughts turned to the unusual snakedoctors he had seen that day. He closed his eyes as the forest played a strange, almost rhythmic symphony that began to soothe his mind, and he laid down and fell asleep.

As the early morning light penetrated his makeshift shelter, Garruty woke to a faint rustling sound. About a foot from his face was a tiny mouse opossum on one of his bent over saplings, clinging tightly with its teeny feet and pale, hairless tail. When Garruty moved to get a better look, the tiny marsupial nimbly shot up the branch and disappeared.

Garruty sat up, rubbed his eyes and stretched; he was stiff and arthritic from lying on the hard ground. *At least the rain stopped*, he observed. His felt a pain in his left thigh; he reached into his pocket and pulled out two rolls of Smarties.

"Ahhh, I was lying on my lunch," he quipped.

As he crawled out from under his shelter, the trees above rustled and he was showered with large drops of water. He had startled a small troop of monkeys, and as they scrambled through the tree canopy, they shook loose the rainwater that had collected on the leaves during the night. *What an unusual species — protruding face, long orange beards, and black circles around their eyes*, he thought. All of a sudden Garruty felt itchy, and hurriedly began to scratch several reddish welts on his neck and arms.

"Dang, must have gotten nailed by some pretty nasty mosquitoes during the night. I better not scratch'em or like Mom always said, the bumps will turn into sores and get infected."

He wished for a companion. "I've got to find help today, and maybe while I'm looking I can find something, anything, to eat."

He tightened the cap of his precious plastic bottle full of rainwater. He cut a small twig and frayed one end to use as a toothbrush. Despite all his bodily pain, he still couldn't stand the feeling of tartar building up on his teeth. He found an overgrown side path and after a few hundred yards came to a small sandy river. There was still no sign of human habitation, but he reasoned that if he followed the river downstream far enough, he would have to come out somewhere. Just in case he had to come back to his shelter, he broke off a small branch, tore off all the bark, and drove it deep into the sand near the obscure path.

The river looked like a large fluid snake slowly winding through a curvy, lush green hallway. The deepest spots were only about knee-deep, and Garruty had little trouble wading downstream on the firm sand bottom. It wasn't long before he started seeing several brightly colored damselflies hanging on the latticework formed by vines along the shady bank. He also saw some small fish, but they were much too quick to catch. *Hell, even if I caught one, I'd never be able to eat it raw.*

As he scanned the vegetation, hoping to see a bunch of avocados, or a coconut, or even some limes, he noticed a few large, gray-green lizards bearing erect armored plates on their backs lurking on a high sandy bank.

"Geez, they must be at least three feet long, and they look pretty menacing," he fretted. "Think I'll walk the other side for awhile."

He turned and was startled to see a group of large blue and orange snakedoctors skim across the surface of the water and swoop upwards into the branches of a dead, overhanging tree. Garruty's jaw dropped when he saw that the "branch" they lit on started to shake. He then saw that it was a large snake, its sides mottled with dark brown and tan, its underside greenish-yellow. He noticed that blood was dripping from its belly, discoloring the water below. He slowly waded over until he was underneath the tree. He saw several of the large snakedoctors land on the snake's head and fan it with their silver blue wings, while others flew underneath the snake and began to close the gash on its belly. Within minutes, he no longer saw blood leaking out, and the snake became quiet. Several of the snakedoctors that worked on the snake's wound spiraled downward and splashed into the water. Garruty picked one up, and sensed a mild electric jolt; he set them one by one on leaves along the bank. He'd never seen such a large beautiful species. *Sure wish I had a way to keep one of these.* He watched them recuperate and fly downstream. He looked up just in time to see their patient slowly crawl through adjacent branches of the dead tree and disappear.

Garruty took a sip of water and kept wading. As he splashed along, he kept comparing yesterday's snakedoctors and their behavior with what he had just observed. He now had seen three instances of dragonflies helping injured snakes! They were all so amazingly different, but in each instance they came close to death.

As he waded further, his stomach began to growl again, and he remembered the two rolls of Smarties in his side pocket. He slowly crunched and swallowed the little tart, disc-shaped candies he'd saved so long. That made him even hungrier and he picked up the pace.

Before long he saw a small clearing to the left. He cautiously climbed up the bank to see if there was anything edible there. The first thing that caught his eye was a group of stocky, rust-colored birds on the far side of the clearing. They were notably larger than full-grown domestic turkeys. Incredibly, they were munching the leaves of a low bushy plant in their heavy beaks.

"Good grief, where am I? Leaf-eating birds*!*" he gasped.

So as not to spook them, he crouched to stay out of sight. He needed a rest anyway, and this was a pretty entertaining sidelight. All of a sudden the birds looked up simultaneously and turned their beady eyes to the left side of the clearing. Like a flash, a huge bird with outstretched stumpy wings streaked across the small clearing, heading straight for the plant-eaters. Garruty was awe-struck; this powerful bird was at least 6 feet tall and had teeth*!* Plus he was sure there were claws on the front edge of its wings*!* The huge bird was closing in on the heavy-legged plant eaters, and they reacted by clumsily jumping and running into the forest. The predator crashed wildly through the thick vegetation behind them.

Garruty froze.

With the forest now deadly silent, he recalled a TV special describing the fossils of huge, flightless predatory birds and showing an artist's rendition of what they must have looked like. But those birds have been extinct for thousands of years*!* he almost blurted out loud. All the strange things he had seen were now finally adding up to a startling conclusion.

"Did I travel back in time, tens of thousands of years?" he whispered, shaken with the thought. "If that bird was real, and as horrific as the paleontologists speculated, I've got to get back. But how?"

Garruty wished he were the size of a bug, in case that monster came back his way. He stayed at the edge of the river until the sounds of the forest returned. As he carefully made his way back upstream, more aware now of all the strange plants and animals around him, he felt more confused than ever. More and more the surroundings looked like a scene from a time long past. He felt weak, and it took most of the afternoon to get back to the naked branch he had left as a path marker. On the way to his makeshift shelter, he smelled an acrid scent, which after a few minutes he recognized as the territorial mark of a cat. Garruty visualized it was a large cat. Hell, could be a saber tooth, he thought, unsure as he was of what time period he was in.

He snuck over to his shelter, dismantled it and moved it to the base of a large, buttressed tree, closer to the area where he hoped the giant oak drum still was. He then got some mud from the edge of the little stream and rubbed it on his neck, arms and hands to foil any more nasty mosquitoes. By this time it was almost dark. No way I get any sleep tonight, he thought. Soon the blackest cloak he'd ever experienced crept over him, and he sat there staring ahead, seeing nothing, listening keenly, but hearing nothing. He felt grateful about one thing: that infernal tune, "Roll Out The Barrel," had finally left his brain. In its place were new lyrics, such as, "Today has been a sad and lonesome day."

Man, Bob Dylan always pulls me through the hard times; now can he keep me sane too? he wondered. Garruty had always heeded the advice he once read on a bathroom wall: "Don't believe everything you think." Now he wondered, *What happens when you get to the point where you start to doubt everything you think?*

Contrary to his expectation, Garruty did fall asleep that night, though sleep came in short, fitful intervals and he felt more awake than asleep. The only way he knew he had fallen asleep was by the continuing dream. At first he was in a tropical Paradise, where he sat relaxing along a crystal blue lake, and everything was beautiful and clean. But the dream kept changing, and soon he was wandering through a thick jungle, thorny plants tearing his clothes and skin. Hungry predators, such as needle-nosed crocodiles, man-sized therapod dinosaurs, and saber-tooth cats repeatedly tried to ambush him. The third time he fell asleep, his earlier wish to be as small as a bug was fulfilled and he was able to hide from the large predators. But as a plant bug, he encountered a greater number of predators, terrifying insects such as a preying mantis, a beetle with large gnashing mandibles, and an assassin bug. Seeing these bugs on their own level was unnerving, as he witnessed the quick cold-bloodedness of predatory insects, and he judged their existence as unparalleled in the animal kingdom. Throughout the dreams, short rhymes kept popping into his head, such as:

I'm lying here, dying of fear,
trying to fight the bite—
before sunrise I shrink in size and
engage in war with a six-legged carnivore.

The next morning Garruty woke up to a light cool rain; he was tired, sore all over, and really hungry. He sat there for a long time, trying to think clearly. He knew his strength wouldn't hold up much longer. He decided to go back up the hill to the giant oak drum.

"If I really did travel back in time in that thing, it's all I've got to return to the time I came from."

The little path up the hillside was now slipperier than greased owl crap. He hid his camera under his shirt, hoping to keep it dry. In his haste to get up the hill he slipped several times and cut his already bruised knees on a sharp palm branch that lay across the path. The rain had washed most of the mud off his neck and arms. Finally he made it back to the giant drum, just as another heavy downpour began. As he hustled inside that mysterious vessel, wet, worried, and hoping some big snake wasn't in there, a crazy thought popped into his head: I got here by tripping my flash once, maybe two flashes in succession will get me back home! Who am I fooling? But hey, anything is worth a try right now.

As he shifted himself to fit the curve of the drum, out of the corner of his eye he caught a glimpse of something moving toward him, something that looked dappled orange and hairy. Oh man, he thought, do something quick. He knew the batteries in his flash were getting low, and he prayed, Don't fail me now. Then he remembered he was aiming his camera at the inscriptions and strange insect drawings when the damn thing rolled away with him the first time.

"How about trying that again?" he whispered. "Man, I just hope there are two flashes left in these batteries."

His eyes were adjusting to the dim interior of the barrel, but he couldn't find the inscription and drawings. He changed positions and realized he was sitting on them. He propped himself up, crossed his toes and looked through the fogged-up viewfinder. He pressed the shutter release. The unit flashed, and he waited. He felt the giant barrel shake a little. He waited for what seemed like an eternity for the flash unit to recycle. When the little green light finally came on, he thought no guts, no glory. He pressed the shutter release again, and in a moment of optimism, braced himself. After a few seconds, the giant barrel shuddered again and then began to roll, slowly at first, then picking up speed. He took a peek, expecting to see flashing lights, but it was totally black. He was losing ability to sense anything, and all he could think was, This is what it must be like entering a black hole.

He couldn't estimate how long the old barrel rolled, or if it was going downhill, uphill, or anywhere for that matter. But he knew when it stopped! When it rolled against the buttressed roots of a large beech tree, it tilted and flipped over, spilling its contents like a sack of apples. He staggered up and out of some briars—he was back in Arkansas!

Garruty gathered himself by holding his shaking hands together and blew a sigh of relief. He picked up his backpack and followed the path back the way he had come just three days earlier.

"Seems like weeks since I was here," he muttered. After about an hour of slow hiking, he found his old van where he had parked it. His key ring was still in a side pocket of his backpack, so he slid the key in the ignition, gave it a turn and heard the motor come to life. He finally started to relax. He stopped at a clear stream, stripped off all his clothes and dove in. After a few minutes of bathing, he shouted, "I'm so hungry I could eat hospital waste!"

He pulled up to the first country diner he came across and ordered a barbeque plate with cole slaw, French fries, and iced tea. For desert he had his favorite, vanilla ice cream covered with caramel sauce. The trip back to Alabama was interrupted only by stops to get bottled water. Before he got home, however, he started to feel an upset stomach, muscle aches and a slow-building headache. He soon experienced a fever, then chills. *Must have been something I ate at that diner*, he thought.

As soon as he got home, he drank more water and flopped down on the couch. His temperature fluctuated rapidly over the next 24 hours. He fell into a coma-like sleep, which was interrupted by several trips to the bathroom.

When he awoke the next day, the fever and chills lessened and he wasn't shaking much anymore. He went outside to sleep in his favorite hammock. After another day of rest, he began to feel better, but he noticed a bunch of new mosquito bites on his legs and elbows.

"Dad-gum Asian tiger mosquitoes must have been drilling me while I was asleep in the hammock," he mumbled. "They must be thick already. And my grass is high enough to hide a giraffe." He decided mowing could wait at least another day.

As he began to feel better, he decided to postpone the difficult study on insect distributions. It was more inviting to dwell on what he saw on his trip back in time. Garruty was well aware that most educated folks knew that snakedoctors (also called snakecharmers) do not tend to sick snakes or even associate with snakes in any way. Indeed, entomologists, those who study bugs inside and out, expressly rejected this idea as unfounded long ago, burying it in the scrap heap of nineteenth-century generated superstitions.

But the observations Garruty made on his trip led him to suspect that maybe dragonflies did nurse snakes back to health, or at least had done so in their evolutionary past. Hadn't he just seen them heal up snakes and take great risk doing so, often becoming injured themselves, only to be left behind by the selfish reptiles? Even so, Garruty decided not to tell anyone either about the snakedoctors' strange behavior or his adventure with the giant oak drum for that matter. He thought it over for days. *If I tell people that snakedoctors heal snakes, there will be all-out war on these poor insects. Snakes have been persecuted for ages, almost beyond belief, and I'm not going to be responsible for any similar level of condemnation of snakedoctors. And traveling back in time? No one will believe that one.*

There was one other reason he didn't come forward—his photographs were ruined. Every frame was streaked with bright yellow and green, leaving him without tangible proof of the snakedoctors or the giant oak drum. He often thought about trying to go back to that time-travel barrel, maybe going forward in time by tripping the flash three times. The thought of seeing the insects of the future was mighty tempting. But the uncertainty of that transportation system was too foreboding for him. Still, the urge to tell anyone who wanted to give it a try for themselves where to find that GOD-awful barrel was hard to suppress.

2

The Stance of the Ants

Garruty got home late on May 24th and was almost sleepwalking by the time he got to the door and pulled the mail out of the box. He had spent the entire day in the field looking for signs of interaction between dragonflies and snakes, hoping to see some sign of "snakedoctor" behavior, but had no luck.

"You shouldn't have stayed out all day, you old fool," he scolded himself.

He was still weak from the "Arkansas food poisoning" episode, plus he was tired from mowing the lawn the day before. Stepping inside the house, the darkness and quiet reminded him he lived alone. He resigned himself to another lonely night. Oh well, I'm getting horizontal as soon as I can anyway.

He put out some cat food, warmed up some leftover pizza for supper, took a shower and finally crashed on the couch.

"Ahhh, this is good, Tinker," he murmured to his little gray sidekick as she piled onto the blanket. Her purring seemed more pronounced than usual.

After a relaxing minute, Garruty turned on his side and saw the pile of mail he had plopped down on the nearby end table. On top of the stack was an official looking letter addressed to "Mr. Garruty." He put on his reading glasses, opened the envelope, and found a summons ordering him to appear before the High Court of the Formicidae on May 28th.

"That's Memorial Day! I was really looking forward to a quiet day in the hammock," he muttered. "What the heck can this be about?" Then he figured it out. "These must be the ants living on the slope near the steps that lead to my backyard, Tinker. I wouldn't have thought they were the feisty type, but they're claiming that I ran over their home with my lawn mower on May 22nd, killing 13 of their family, young ones included, and inflicting major damage to the architecture surrounding their nest and some of their top galleries." At the bottom of the page it said ON THE TOP TEN MOST WANTED LIST. Garruty realized that somebody was pulling a prank on him, and tomorrow he would find out whom. But what he needed right then was a good night's sleep.

Too soon, through narrow eye slits, Garruty sensed the early morning light streaming through the living room window.

"How could morning get here so fast? It seems like I just fell asleep!"

He got up, slower than usual, and splashed cold water in his face.

"Think I'll bring the paper in before we have breakfast, Tinker," he whispered to the little cat.

He stepped outside, oblivious to everything. As he closed the door and turned toward the yard, there right in front of him was a huge mound of dirt with a large hole in the center. He suddenly realized that he was cornered by three huge army ant soldiers, each bigger than him! Without warning, they simultaneously clicked their long sickle-like mandibles around him. The one behind him clamped his jaws around his shoulders, pinning his arms to his sides, the one on his left grabbed him by the waist, and the other one wrapped his jaws around his legs. He was helplessly immobilized. Without hesitation, they scurried down the hole and threw him into a damp, dark cell hidden in the deeper recesses of their subterranean world.

He sat there on cool, damp earth, shaken but trying to contemplate the situation. Could it be? I vaguely remember mowing that grassy little hillside. There was a small bare spot, and it seemed that in the center there was some soil piled up around a small hole in the ground. Yes, I remember it, though I know I didn't realize that it was an anthill until my mower had already passed over it. Although Garruty didn't pay much attention to it at the time, he knew it was possible that the blade of the mower scraped the top of that little mound. Could he have done as much damage as stated in that summons?

He feverishly tried to build his defense case, playing out all possible arguments and counter arguments. He knew what hard workers ants were, and therefore expected that their prosecutors would be prepared for just about anything. His first line of defense would be based on property ownership. This is my land, and I have a deed to prove it. Those ants are trespassers, squatters, nay, invaders of my land! Then he thought, Wait, I cannot assume that my deed will have any standing in their court. Hmmm, they probably have a deed proving ownership of that 3" mound of ground. Besides, I don't think trespassing is grounds for murder.

He decided to turn the tables on them. Those ants raped the land surrounding their mound. Did they submit an Environmental Impact Statement? It is amply evident from the devastation of the landscape surrounding their dwelling that they have no regard for the environment. Their activities lead to a loss of biological diversity and erosion, undoubtedly unlawful in any society! But the realization struck him that he could be assuming too much. They could easily expect this argument and produce legal documents defending their hunter-gatherer existence.

Garruty searched for another approach, some argument that could swing the Judge and Jury in his favor. I finally have it! There were no signs to warn me that spot was inhabited. Without knowledge of their presence, it was an accident!

But the ants' lawyers could quickly counter. "The mounded up soil surrounding the entrance was in plain sight, and this is a well-known, even universal, sign of occupancy. Ignorance leads to negligence and is no excuse before the court!"

He had an aching feeling they would also claim that it was obvious before the court that the defendant could not read.

He searched his reeling mind for hours and couldn't really come up with what seemed like a solid defense. There were so many unknowns that he decided to wing it. He suddenly noticed that the air was dank and smelled sweet, almost like honey. As his eyes adjusted, he could make out the rough texture of the dirt walls of this tomb. His mind clawed, Is this happening? Am I real anymore? He felt he had no sense of time; all he knew was that he was getting cold and more worried. He couldn't think; he knew he was drifting but he didn't care anymore.

Suddenly he awoke to a screeching announcement: "It's Reckoning Time!!"

He thought, It must be Memorial Day.

The huge soldiers returned, picked him up in their jaws as before and shuffled him upward through crooked tunnels and into a large, dimly lit room. This must be their courtroom, he reasoned to himself as he was rudely shoved down onto a little pile of dirt. He scanned the room—it was completely packed with ants, at least a dozen species, countless thousands of individuals. He saw the Jury on his right—144 worker ants, perched in 12 ascending rows, their elbowed antennae simultaneously bobbing up and down. First up would go all the left ones as down went all the right ones, then the right ones up and the left ones down, as if calculating, and all the while their cold eyes riveted on him, examining his very being. This was an impartial jury? This was going to be a fair trial?

Then she entered the courtroom. The Judge was without a doubt the biggest, most furious-looking thing he had ever seen. Her black robe veiled most of her shining black body, but didn't hide her hideous stinger, which seemed to have a pulse and mind of its own; he felt it knew exactly where he was. All the other ants froze upon her entrance and there was a menacing silence. The little red ant sitting next to him, obviously his appointed defense counsel, gave him an awfully nervous glance.

Garruty tried to sink into his pile of dirt, thinking, I should have been given the opportunity to hire a really good lawyer, an ant from a neighboring hill, one with a law degree and a "Clarence Darrow" reputation. At least I should have gotten a big one!

The Judge, perched high above all, twitched her right antenna at the soldier ants. These warriors, with huge sickles protruding from the sides of their mouths, came over and instantly tore his little red lawyer to shreds. Horrified, he tilted his head downward, thinking a submissive posture was his only hope for survival. After a moment of silence he looked up. The Judge pointed her left antenna at the Jury; they simultaneously rose and screamed "GUILTY!!"

"What!?" Garruty cried. "I haven't even had a chance to tell my side!"

The Judge pointed her stinger at him and exclaimed, "Silence! Killing has no defense. Now your sentence!"

He thought, Why am I just sitting here taking this? Why don't I get up and bust out of here? Ummm, he reminded himself, instant death is quite a deterrent to flight.

Then the Judge turned toward him and in a low, hollow, vibrating voice exclaimed "I am impressed with what a cold-blooded killer you are. You would be a perfect fit in our society. You must be our King!!"

Garruty was shocked at this turn-around. The ants admired him! He suddenly realized what it meant to be on their Most Wanted List. Then the reality of it hit him and fired the thought into his brain, Spend the rest of my life here with the ants?? Whoa.

After a moment, he responded to the Judge, "I'll need a little time to think about it."

She squared herself and glowered at him, but at that precise moment a brilliant light flashed through the courtroom, followed almost instantaneously by an ear-drum splitting clap of thunder. Throughout the courtroom ants nervously started to move, and within seconds muddy water began to flood across the floor of the ominous cavern. The liquid danger sent ants scrambling in all directions, and chaos was on. That this might be his chance to escape did not elude Garruty's traumatized brain, and he leaped for the exit hole. The steep, slippery sides made it difficult for him to ascend that doorway to freedom, and worse yet a group of smaller soldier ants noticed his attempt and they began to attack him. As their needle-like stingers were penetrating his chest, he looked up, the rain pelting his face. He closed his eyes and grabbed the top edge of the hole. As he pulled himself up, he opened his eyes, and hey! There he was on his couch, his little gray cat busily kneading his chest with her sharp little claws. What painful relief!

As he sat up, he noticed his hair was wet and there was mud on his hands and knees. His little gray cat sniffed him.

"Oh Tinker, it's so good to see you! Geez, I need to get away for awhile," he declared. "C'mon, help me pack. It's time to visit some folks up in Illinois and Wisconsin."

He pulled out a medium-sized luggage bag and opened it up. As Garruty was packing, Tinker played hide-and-seek in the bag, jumping at imaginary wild things. She must know that every time I walk out the door with those bags, it'll be lonely here for a while, he thought. He finished by dropping some insect books, other references, and his stack of field notebooks in a box. Just before noon he was ready to leave. He petted Tinker, then picked her up, gave her a hug, and set her down. Then he took a real close look at his front yard, flashing his eyes left and right before he stepped out.

3

The Wasp Sting

As he drove north into western Tennessee, Garruty was still mentally regurgitating his recent bug encounters, wondering if his ability to separate reality and fantasy was fading. Needing to stretch and calm his mind for a while, he pulled off the highway at Clifton and walked down by the big river. This area of the Tennessee River had always been one of his favorite places, a sanctum full of natural beauty and serenity. He walked along the sandy riverbank, breathing in a light mix of fish and algae smells exhaled by the semi-healthy river. A bald eagle soared upriver, though it looked paradoxically tiny in the distance. Males of several kinds of songbirds were singing from their secluded vantage points in the tangled bushes growing high along the vertically cut riverbank, marking their territories for the impending mating season. He couldn't hear higher pitches that well anymore, but he crudely mocked their tunes and felt flattered when they answered, as if he were their main competitor.

Simplistically direct in their intentions, like pure unwrapped desire. I had a melody once, if not a song, he thought.

Suddenly he felt small waves splash up on his weathered running shoes as he slowly stepped along the flat, sand-gravel edge. He looked down to see how close he was to the water and noticed several insect skins on the sand by his feet. He put on his reading glasses and took a closer look, his excitement building. He carefully picked one up and quickly realized that some type of large Clubtail dragonfly had recently emerged here, leaving these empty hulls behind when they metamorphosed to the adult stage; he suspected it was something interesting, hopefully a species valuable to his studies. He quickly gathered several of them, put them in a plastic vial, and walked briskly back toward the boat ramp from which he had started his leisurely walk.

Garruty sat down on his favorite large rock to take a good look at the fragile dragonfly skins. After a few minutes of intense gazing through his hand lens, he was sure he had happened upon one of the 'impossible-to-find' species he had been in quest of for years. The nymphs must inhabit this special, narrow part of the big river, probably burrowing in the bottom sands where conditions are just right for them, he thought.

He looked out over the wide river and imagined the swift black and yellow females darting low over the surface, tapping their abdomens and releasing hundreds of tiny, cream-colored eggs. He wished he knew how to dive so he could try to find the nymphs in the river bottom. Just then a large piece of driftwood floated into view and his thoughts began to drift. He thought about how alone he was, and how much he missed his ex-wife, Adele. She'd left him 10 years ago, maybe more. After 20 years of marriage, though age had changed her slightly, she still looked as fantastic to him as the day they met. When he closed his eyes he could see her long chestnut hair, long eyelashes, and shapeliness; he could smell her perfume. Not thinking about the dragonfly skins anymore, he set the plastic vial and his hand lens in a large fissure in the rock and leaned back with his hands clasped over his left knee. Before she walked out on him, she had been telling him that she needed more than just tagging along on bug-chasing field trips. He had been beating himself up for years, knowing that he didn't take Adele's warnings seriously enough until it was too late. But how she fell for another woman he still could not fathom. Adele met Gwen at a party in New York just when he and Adele were going through a bad time. Right after their divorce, Adele moved to the Big Apple, and as far as he knew, she was still living with that battleaxe.

A distant rumbling brought Garruty back to the present. Dark clouds were building up in the west, moving toward him like huge bowling balls rolling down a lane that was the river. Not far away a sharp bolt of lightning split the sky. Garruty thought that if the next bolt hit the rock he was perched on, a lot of problems would be solved. All of a sudden, heavy raindrops pelted down and a survival instinct overwhelmed him.

Guess I'm not so different from bugs after all, he thought. Better get movin'.

Continuing on the drive north, Garruty felt bad about leaving Tinker at home, but she wasn't a good traveler. It wasn't that long ago that he left her alone for the Arkansas trip. That thought reminded him of the wild experience with the GOD-awful barrel. He quickly shifted his thoughts away from it. Cats are great companions, he thought. Sometimes he felt that Tinker was his only friend. But this time he planned to be away for an indefinite length of time. All of a sudden he realized he'd been driving for miles without seeing the highway or anything he passed. He tried in vain to focus on driving.

He tried to comfort himself. Aw, Mandy will take good care of Tink. She lives just across the street. I just hope she can stay and play with her for awhile every day.

Garruty knew that staying home right then wouldn't be good for him. Too many weird things were happening to him. He still wasn't sure those ants were a dream; they seemed so real. He needed to talk to someone in confidence, and he couldn't think of anyone better than his old colleague at the University of Illinois, Dr. Jackson P. Bartley. Jasper. It's been over a year since I've seen that old curmudgeon.

It was near dusk when Garruty entered southern Illinois. The dimming sky and the barrage of insects that had splattered his windshield, leaving numerous large, yellowish orange streaks right in his field of vision, were taxing his ability to keep the old Chevy van on the road. Sure need to clean this windshield; I need to gas up too, he thought. He exited where there were several signs advertising gas stations and motels. He pulled into a Shell station, filled the gas tank and got most of the bug grease off his windshield. I sure hate that so many butterflies and other harmless insects get smacked on the highway, he lamented.

Feeling tired, Garruty decided to stop and get a motel room. Unfortunately, not one of the four motels at that exit had a vacancy. After striking out at the fourth motel, he remembered seeing a sign for Foxhole State Park before the exit. He went back to the gas station to ask the attendant how to get to the park.

The big-lipped, anemic-looking red haired kid said, "Iz jis 67 mals out far sen."

"What? I'm not driving no 67 miles to camp!" he replied, cupping his right ear with his hand.

"No, 6 or 7 miles," the kid shouted.

"Oh. Which way?

"East, on 47!" the kid bellowed.

"OK, I hear ya," Garruty replied. He bought a sandwich wrapped in cellophane, snacks and bottled water, and headed east on County Road 47.

It was pitch dark when Garruty got to Foxhole State Park. He picked out a campsite, placed $8 for a non-hookup site in the little envelope provided at the unmanned gatehouse and slipped it through the narrow metal slot. Instead of setting up his tent he decided he would just sleep in the van; he always carried a bedroll for occasions such as this. As he sat on the picnic bench and ate his sandwich, he looked up at the black, star-studded sky. He saw a meteor streak overhead to the northeast.

"That's how life is," he sighed, "a brief flurry, sometimes not so bright." The melancholy moment abruptly ended. "Ouch" he yelped as he slapped his neck. "Now what's biting me?"

Soon he was being bitten on the face, hands and ankles. He scuttled to the van and clambered in, but some of the hungry horde slipped in with him. He groped around and found his flashlight. Flicking it on, he could see several dozen of the agile little hypodermic needles floating around in the back of the van. He resigned himself to whacking them as they landed and drilled into his skin. When he finished his sandwich, it occurred to him that he had forgotten to get some Smarties in the gas station food mart. He munched some potato chips for dessert. When he brushed his teeth, he rolled down the window and quickly spit out the narrow opening to keep as many mosquitoes from getting in as possible. He made a few entries in his journal and then finally lay down to read for a while. Every few minutes he had to stop and swat a mosquito. Around 10:00 he dozed off, a distant high-pitched whine still in his ears.

Garruty was awake at sunrise. Before he stepped outside to relieve his full bladder, he sprayed some repellent on his arms and neck. Nonetheless, at the edge of his campsite, a bloodthirsty reserve squadron attacked him.

"Man, I'm outa here!" he screamed. Guess that repellent is pretty old, he thought. He scratched red welts all the way to Champaign-Urbana.

"Hey Pancake, what are you doing here?" Jasper greeted him with a big smile as Garruty pulled into his driveway. "Geez, it's been awhile! Still got some hair I see."

"Yeah, and I see you're still pregnant," Garruty shot back through his open window.

Jasper giggled and rubbed his burgeoning belly. "Yep. Hey, go on in, the door's open. I have to go over to the department for a late staff meeting, last minute budget changes. So make yourself at home, I'm not sure what time I'll be back."

"Look Jasper, I don't want to just sit around. I need to talk to you, but until you get back home, can I just go over to the department and look through the insect collection?"

"Yeah, sure. Do you remember how to get to Claxton Hall? It's kind of late, but it should still be open."

"I think so. Don't worry about me. I'll see you tonight."

Jasper jumped in his jeep and tore out of the driveway, in his usual rush. Garruty put his bag inside the house and took a shower. He locked the door as he left. Jasper's wife had left him long before Adele left Garruty. Garruty wondered if there was an entomologist anywhere who had a marriage that lasted. As he headed toward the University of Illinois campus, he thought about Jasper. They had attended graduate school together at Florida and had kept in touch for the 35 years since then. Though they were good friends, sometimes Garruty felt that things Jasper said could be taken two ways. Most of the time, he wasn't sure if Jasper was kidding or serious. It put doubts in his mind about their relationship and also about his own status in the scientific community. The limerick Jasper wrote right after Garruty published an extensive paper on rates of food uptake and excretion in insects especially came to mind. The words still haunted him:

Now the fellow who studies bug feces,
Must have slipped beyond simple neuroses;
For a brain must be lame,
To make that claim to fame;
Could it be he's advanced to psychoses?

How could they print derision like that in the most prominent entomological newsletter in the United States? Garruty wondered. He wanted to believe that Jasper was just having fun and it got out of hand. He sensed that their relationship changed after that little episode. Being an introvert, Garruty had never confronted Jasper about it when they went on field trips together or when they saw each other at meetings. But he still liked Jasper. Jasper had a way of making sense of just about anything, and right now, that was what Garruty was wanting.

Preoccupied with that awkward experience, Garruty almost drove past the main entrance to the University. He got a parking permit and started walking in the direction of the Entomology Department. When he got to Claxton, he didn't recognize much of it. It had been a long time since Garruty had been there, and since then the university had refurbished and added onto the mammoth building. He pushed open the large glass doors and entered the lobby. The directory on the wall indicated that the Entomology Department was to his right, in the Molecular Biology wing. It appeared that the university had expanded old Claxton in order to accommodate several different biological science disciplines. With no receptionist on duty, he decided to see if he could find the entomology labs on his own. About halfway down the main hallway, he came to two intersecting corridors. There was an old sign on the wall that said Entomology, but nothing to indicate which corridor to take. He decided to try the left hallway first. He passed several large double doors that were labeled in sequence, beginning with Lab M231, but they were locked. A little further down the hall he saw lights coming from underneath the doors of Lab M244 and decided to see if there was anyone there who could give him directions to the Insect Collection.

The room looked like an extensive chemistry lab, lined with shelves of glassware and chemicals. One large lab bench had a strange apparatus in which some chemical reaction was taking place. He could hear muffled voices coming from somewhere in the back, perhaps an office. As he made his way toward the rear of the lab, he saw several large screen cages. Inside each cage was a huge paper wasp nest. Some of the colonies were composed of thousands of wasps. I must be near the right place, Garruty thought.

As he approached the concealed office in the back of the lab, he heard a rather high-pitched voice with an Arab accent.

"What good is it to develop super wasp venom if we can't deliver it to kill Americans? The attack date is almost here. We don't have much time. We'll have to release the wasps if you can't solve the problem of how to deliver the toxin."

Garruty could hardly believe what he just heard. Maybe I'm not in the right place, he thought.

A deeper voice with a slightly different accent replied, "It's not that easy, Faysal. Somehow the toxin has to be injected into the blood stream, you can't just put it in their drinking water. The venom is quickly broken down by gastric juices and would have little effect. That's why we've been..." There was a pause. "Shhhh, did you hear something?"

Garruty had bumped into a rack of glass tubes as he inched closer to the office door in order to hear their conversation better. He ducked behind the lab bench, but there was no place to hide. Just as the two subversives came out of the office and started in Garruty's direction, the lab doors burst open. In rushed a team of FBI agents and policemen wearing gas masks. Inside the lab, they split into smaller squads and infiltrated the whole room.

"Freeze! Get your arms up!" the agent in charge hollered when he spotted the two chemical terrorists. They quickly complied, being unarmed. Policemen took the two suspects into custody, handcuffing them and then taking them out separately.

"Anyone else in here?" asked the lead agent.

One of the squads found Garruty hunkered down by the far lab bench. "Here's another one, Agent Booker, hiding behind this lab bench, but he looks like an American," a uniformed Swat team member shouted.

"Handcuff him and bring him over here," replied Booker.

Just then, several of the large wasps stung three of the law enforcement officers. The men had accidentally torn a slit in the side of one of the cages when they rushed into the lab. One of the officers fell to the floor. "Masks on, everybody! Damn! Secure this area and start looking for chemical weapons. And signs of Anthrax. And get those germ warfare experts in here," Booker ordered. FBI Special Agent Stan Booker was of medium height and build, with slick black hair and a rough complexion. His large black eyes could be menacing, but they were also capable of showing compassion. He was authoritative and looked wise beyond his years.

"OK mister, what's your name?"

"Garruty. Amos P. Garruty. Look, I..."

Booker interrupted. "I'll ask the questions here. What's your role in this? We've had this operation under surveillance for months now, and got no mention of an American being involved."

"I am not involved in any..." began Garruty, but he was interrupted by a woman and two men in white coats, also wearing gas masks.

"Bio warfare experts reporting, sir."

"All right, Ms. Metler, let's see if you can use that pretty head for something besides looking at. Get started examining every square inch of this place, and if you find anything suspicious, anything that might be Anthrax, let me know immediately," ordered Booker. He turned around and inadvertently put his hand near a wasp perched on the edge of the lab bench. "Eee-youch," he yelped. Within seconds his hand swelled and turned red. "Damn it, now I get stung in my sore hand. What the hell are these wasps doing in here? I've never seen wasps so aggressive."

Garruty spoke up. "They're not making Anthrax. They're making some kind of super-duper wasp venom."

"What? What makes you say that?" asked Booker, squinting, trying to endure the pain.

Garruty explained why he was there and told him about the conversation he'd overheard, especially the part about the problems the terrorists were having figuring out how to deliver the venom to their victims en masse. He pointed to the large screened cages.

"See, they've obviously colonized these insects and analyzed their venom, probably for mass production of synthetic venom."

Agent Booker questioned Garruty for a while longer. He was inclined to believe his story, but he told Garruty that he was still under suspicion and that they were taking him in for further questioning and fingerprinting. He then called his office, ordering a search for a top organic chemist to investigate the possibility of this potential biological threat.

Garruty offered, "You need to get an entomologist with expertise in Hymenoptera too, to find out what kind of wasps those are."

At the police station, Garruty was fingerprinted and then questioned for over an hour. He was allowed one phone call, which he placed to Jasper. He explained his dilemma and it wasn't long before Jasper showed up. "How did you get into this mess in the first place, Pancake?" was Jasper's first question.

"I couldn't find the section where the Insect Collection is housed, and I went into that lab to ask for help," he informed Jasper. "I 'luckily' stumbled into a terrorist plot! And an FBI sting!!" he added. Turning to Agent Booker, he asked, "Can we go now? I'm exhausted," he added.

"Yeah, but I may need to talk to you some more tomorrow, so I would suggest not leaving the city yet," said Booker weakly. His hand and arm were terribly swollen, and he obviously was in severe pain.

Jasper took his beleaguered friend home, fixed a light salad for him, and tried to help him relax. They talked for a while, mainly about the excitement Garruty just went through. Garruty also described his travel back in time and the dream about the ants taking him to court, emphasizing how he seemed to be struggling with reality. Jasper told him that people with lively imaginations often have those kinds of experiences, but they would pass. They finished up rehashing some old times and then hit the sack.

The next morning went slowly, as the two old friends waited around the house in case the police called. Garruty showed Jasper one of the dead wasps; he had almost forgotten about it. He had slipped it in an envelope and hidden it in his shirt pocket during all the commotion in the lab the night before. It was over an inch long with reddish orange wings and an abdomen patterned in blue and yellow spots separated by red arrow-shaped stripes. The stinger was longer than any other they had seen. After studying it for over an hour, the two old entomologists were unable to identify it; they were sure they had never seen it before. Jasper, having studied wasps for most of his career, hypothesized that it might be a genetically engineered hybrid, possibly the two parent species coming from some eastern Asian country or nearby islands. Jasper had also researched the chemical complexity of wasp and bee venom in his career, and he knew that such venoms were extremely complex and had never been synthesized before.

That afternoon Jasper called the police. They told him Dr. Garruty was free to go on his way. They also told him that Agent Booker was in intensive care in the hospital, being treated for a severe reaction to the wasp sting he received, as were the three other officers that were stung. They asked if he would come in and assist in handling the wasps and with the chemical analysis of an amber liquid they found stored in ampules in lab M244. Jasper agreed to be there that afternoon. More than that, though, he wanted Garruty to stay longer. But Garruty felt he would be too nervous there, and he really wanted to get on the road. He thanked Jasper for his hospitality and especially for his help. As he got in his van and headed toward the highway, he yelled back at Jasper, "Good luck with your study of the venom. Oh yeah, and let me know if you have a girl or a boy!"

4

The Great Mosquito Festival

Garruty felt some relief after he left Illinois and drove north into central Wisconsin. He decided to take some leisure time before visiting friends and relatives. He spent a few days stopping at various places, observing dragonflies and clearing his mind. This was difficult, as he couldn't help but think about the terrorists and the wasps, Jasper's cooperative study with the authorities, and whether the FBI agents would be all right.

It was Thursday before he made it to the north central part of the state. As darkness began to envelop the western sky on that cool June day, a doe jumped in front of his old Chevy van. He swerved sharply to the right and missed the deer, just barely, but he slammed into the ditch and bashed his head on the steering wheel. When he came to, he felt a bump on his forehead and a few other aches. He grabbed the steering wheel again, put the van in reverse and spun back onto the highway. After about a mile, the van began to overheat. Luckily just then he saw a road sign indicating that Catawba was one mile away. He slowed down as he approached the east edge of the little town and saw an old-fashioned Mobil sign still lit. His hopes rose.

Maybe it's still open. Looks like the kind of place that would have a mechanic who can fix this old tin can. He hoped his trip would be only slightly delayed, as he had also promised to visit his sister in Eagle River. He rolled up to the tiny station, steam billowing up from under the hood, and was relieved to see that the door was open.

Garruty stepped inside the poorly lit station but didn't see anyone who looked like they worked there. Several elderly men were sitting on some badly worn, stained wooden chairs along the left wall. They didn't seem to notice his entrance, intent as they were on the topic of conversation.

"Skeetoes were so big back then they could walk up and slap a turkey in the face," quipped a heavy little man with shaggy white eyebrows, a plump white mustache and bags under his eyes.

The fellow sitting nearest him was taller and lankier. His long-sleeved, light blue shirt was so slack Garruty wondered if there was anything but bones underneath. The man peered out from his stained ball cap, pulled down so far it made his ears stick out, and countered, "Yep, and they had to duck when they barged into the dog house. Dadgum things took off with the puppies."

There was a pause and they both looked over at the oldest looking of the three. Garruty quickly surmised that here was the king of the storytellers at Oscar's Mobil

Station. The man was quite stout and looked as though he'd never smiled. His small dark eyes spent most of their time peering from the corners of his eye sockets. Framed by deep wrinkles that resembled furrows in a hilly field, they made him look shifty.

"What you got to say, Otto?" asked the lanky man.

There was a slight pause. "Worst I ever seen skeetoes was when I worked in the timber camps up North. So thick they had squadrons coming at you in shifts," Otto piped in, as if awakening from a coma. He added, "Met some Air Force pilots who flew over the UP; they said something big showed up on their radar screens. They figured it was a giant mosquito; they heard there was one so big up there it was killing animals by sucking up all their blood."

Just then a rather short, stocky man, his clothes stained with grease and oil, came in through a narrow back doorway wiping his hands with a greasy rag; he headed for the small soda machine by the front door. He dropped a coin in the slot, slid a small bottle of Coke through the metal frame maze, and pulled it up through the metal jaws. It vaguely occurred to Garruty that that type of soda machine dated back to an earlier period. He was thinking that all of them would have been replaced with newer machines, but he lost his thought when Oscar quickly popped the cap off, took a swig and asked, "Can I help you?"

Garruty told him how he had veered off the road and slammed into the ditch, which apparently caused his van to begin to overheat.

"It'll have to wait till morning, I got to finish them bearings in Swede's John Deere B, and it's gettin' late," Oscar quickly informed him.

"Ughh," moaned Garruty, then pleaded, "Is there a place in town I can stay? I don't know anyone here."

Turning toward the tall, lanky yarn spinner, Oscar said "No hotel around here. Hey Ted, can you take him over to Johnny's and see if he's got a spare bed for the night?"

Ted got up, closed his eyes and nodded, and shuffled toward the door with his shoulders hunched over. Garruty started to follow, then turned and asked Oscar, "What time do you open?"

"About seven," he answered. Otto was still mumbling something about the mosquitoes in upper Michigan. As Garruty went out the door, he noticed that the coin slot in the little red Coke machine said "5¢."

They crossed the street, which was actually U.S. Highway 8, and angled over toward Johnny's tavern. There were a few old cars and a scratched, dented-in pickup parked in front; the jukebox playing low, the crack of pool balls and the laughter sifting out the door were inviting sounds. Ted said, "Go on in, Johnny will fix ya up. I'm goin' 'round back, it's about time for the horseshoe tournament to start."

Inside the little tavern the smell of beer, liquor and salty snacks wafted over Garruty as strongly as the air of a warm humid evening on the Gulf Coast. He stepped up to the bar and sat down on a barstool. "What'll ya have buddy?" asked one of the friendliest voices Garruty had ever heard. The barkeep's round face, with his big eyes and little mustache, made Garruty believe he'd been smiling all his life.

"I see you got Miller on tap," Garruty replied; "are you Johnny?"

"Yep. One Miller comin' right up."

Johnny set a 9 oz. glass of cold beer in front of Garruty, who laid down a five-dollar bill. Johnny picked up the bill, turned and rang up the cash register and then laid Garruty's change down on the bar — $4.85. Garruty thought "What, 15¢ for a beer!? Well, I guess if you can get a soda up here for a nickel, you can get a beer for 15¢." Garruty sucked down the beer quickly, ordered another, and asked Johnny if he had a place he could stay for the night. Johnny said he could have the cot in the back of the tavern, and Garruty decided it would have to do. He then asked about the horseshoe tournament out back.

"Go see for yourself," Johnny said. "Make sure you watch ole Ted — he throws the shoes with all his might, and they go just the exact distance between the stakes."

Garruty had to nimbly waltz past stacked cases of Blatz, Schlitz and other makes of beer in a narrow, dark hallway to get to the back door of the tavern. The air had turned remarkably chilly in the short time since sundown, and Garruty shivered a bit as he stepped toward the open backyard. There was Ted under the floodlight, a mere skeleton in work shirt and overhauls, aiming his horseshoe, and when he flung it, sure enough as hard as he could, the shoe made one perfect revolution and softly settled around the far stake. "Ringer!" shouted his partner from the pit where the shoe landed.

Johnny's pot-bellied brother Emil turned to Oliver, a giant of a man, and said, "How 'bout that guy! That's game."

Garruty looked over to the dimly lit side where several onlookers were seated in lawn chairs, including the other two men from Oscar's service station. He went over and offered, "Anybody need a beer or a bottle of pop? I'll buy."

The little man with the white eyebrows and mustache said, "You're money's no good here, friend, this round's on me. By the way, my name's Herman." He reached into a large metal tub, pulled out several icy bottles of Miller High Life and handed one to Garruty.

Garruty thanked him over the clanking of a horseshoe against a metal stake. "My name's Amos Garruty. I heard ya'll talking about skeeters over at the Mobil station. Pretty good yarns, especially what you had to say about the giant one in the U. P." Garruty peered over at Otto.

Otto returned the glance. "Look, maybe Herman and Ted were putting on a bit, trying to outdo one another, but I was serious about part of what I said. There was an account of a giant skeeter up there."

Garruty could sense that this was no time to dispute his new acquaintance, and continued. "I once heard a tale about a man who lived in Michigan years ago. His name was Porter Hutson. There was a legend about his battle with a giant mosquito on the shore of Lake Huron. I can recite it for you, if you wish."

"How 'bout it everybody, want to hear it?" asked Herman.

Everybody chimed in, "For sure."

Garruty found a small wooden stool and sat down in front of the group. At this he noticed that the horseshoe pits became silent, and so he began with purpose "This is the story of 'The Battle of Hutsonwatha!'"

"By the shores of Itchee-Gloomee,
By the shining big lake water,
Flew the terrible piercing insect,
Flew the terrible Aedes,
From the dark and dreadful Hades,
Flew with two wings over the water,
Over the trees the dreadful buzzing,
Left the leaves and branches trembling,
Left fear in the hearts of animals,
Searching for the blood of animals.

Long the people of Mishigama
Heard the stories of piercing insect,
How the terrible Aedes,
Stalked the Deer and the Wabasso,
Sensed them from their place of hiding,
Flew on wings of drumming lace,
To pierce their hearts and take their blood,
Take their souls to the place of Hades,
And feed the children of Aedes,
To come in anger for the people.

So it was that Porter Hutson,
Went before all Mishigama,
Told them he would travel north,
To the rippling big lake water,
To the stronghold of Aedes,
Battle there the piercing insect,
Go to slay the giant insect,
Break its long and piercing beak,
Draw its dark and magic power,
To save the animals and his people.

Far he stalked along the shoreline,
Till darkness came and rest was needed;
Dark around him rose the forest,
Rolled the mist from mighty Huron;
In his sleep he dreamt of insects,
Tiny flying buzzing creatures,
Flying in his ears and nostrils,
Singing songs in unknown language,
Probing him with claws and stinger,
Bringing signs of pain and danger,

When he woke the sky was light,
He felt the rays of the early sun;
Through the mist he saw the water,
Morning glistening on the big still water.
Loud he called to the great Aedes,
A challenge to the piercing insect,
"Here I am, like Ky-rha-no-mus,
Naked before the world of insects,
Barefoot and wielding insect net,
Prepare yourself to meet your doom."

Now the tranquil still-life morning
Filled with the sound of a thunderous drone;
He turned and poised his lacy lance,
Riveting his eyes upon the forest,
When down upon him from above,
Giant legs and wings in turbulence,
Engulfed and pinned him to the ground;
Looking up he saw the huge proboscis,
Stained dark with the blood of others,
Aiming at his heart and soul.

Time suspended like his body,
He stared at the faceted compound eyes,
Cold as steel and unforgiving;
Now he felt the fate of the animals,
Felt the claws and scales, the palps,
Probing for an entry place,
To take away his vital forces;
Stark the realization hit him,
That his very life be taken
To feed the children of piercing insect.

Then the sharp and stabbing beak
Broke and pierced his tender skin,
And as his blood was being taken,
The beginning of the end now on him,
He heard a different thunderous sound,
A greater wind now driven round them,
And from the side a tremendous form
Crashed into the giant Aedes,
Grappled with the piercing insect,
Crunching it with jaws like sickles.

As the colossal Blue-spotted darner,
Bigger than the biggest pine tree,
Took the frightful piercing insect
Far out over the big lake water,
He realized that he had witnessed
What all the people thought a myth;
The protector of the big lake water,
The savior of the animals,
The dragonfly of the big lake water,
Known as Aeshna eremita.

Weak and wounded he gathered strength,
To travel back to show his people
The giant Aedes wings left behind,
And tell about the Great Eremita;
So the people raised their voices,
Rejoiced in the death of Aedes,
Honored all this Porter Hutson,
Called him slayer of Aedes,
Called him saver of the people,
Called him Hutsonwatha."

Garruty looked around at his audience, horseshoe throwers now included. Everyone's eyes were wide open and staring at him. He paused, swigged his beer, then raised his arms and joined his hands behind his head. Several people told him how much they enjoyed the story, and a short fellow named Ralph, missing his two middle teeth, began fumbling out a tune on his old guitar.

Basking in their absolute attention, Garruty added, "I also heard that throughout northern Michigan there is a celebration reenacting the legend of Hutsonwatha that still continues around this time of year, a celebration called 'The Great Mosquito Festival'."

Old Ted finally couldn't hold back and he challenged Garruty, "If you're so interested in it, why haven't you gone up there and seen it for yourself?"

Garrruty retorted, "I might just do that, but the skeetoes up there are so bad. And what if there's one more of those giant ones lurking around up there?"

Everybody shuddered and drank to that.

Otto said, "I'm not taking any chances; no way I'm going up there."

After that, it seemed like everybody had a story or two to tell about mosquitoes. And when they learned that Garruty was an expert on the pesky bugs, it seemed like the questions would never end. He tried to address everybody's concerns, and they let him know how glad they were he dropped in.

By this time, it was after midnight and most of the tavern patrons began to head home. Johnny closed up the tavern and Garruty made up his cot. Although he was uncomfortable at first, he thought it was a lot better than sleeping out in the cool night air. It was warm enough inside the hallway, however, for the mosquitoes that had gotten in through holes in the screen door to find his warm, tasty flesh.

He woke up scratching again. He stumbled his way to the barroom where he saw Johnny cleaning up from the night's activities. The bags under Johnny's eyes made him look tired and a lot older than he did the night before. "Morning. If you're hungry, you can go over to Bugsy's; he whips up a pretty decent breakfast. Wow, looks like the skeeters got you pretty good."

"Yeah, I would have thought it was too cold for 'em."

"I think they get in through that old screen door around dusk; been meaning to get that patched up. Sorry."

"I've been bit before, no big deal. Well, I better go see if Oscar's gotten started fixing my van. Sure was great to meet you. How can I ever thank you for your hospitality?"

Johnny smiled. "No need, you're welcome. Come back and see us if you ever get back this way. By the way, where you headed?"

"Gotta see if they still celebrate the Great Mosquito Festival, and if Hutsonwatha's heroics were real or just a wild tale," replied Garruty.

5

Fireflies in the Great Lakes

As he headed north for Eagle River, Garruty noticed that the van was running better than it had in years. Oscar had not only sealed the cracked radiator and fixed the busted water hose, but he had cleaned the plugs, adjusted the carburetor and put in a new air filter; all that, parts and labor, for $15.32. He had also spilled some Coke on the carpet, but Garruty didn't mind; that would be easy to clean up. He couldn't believe how little the bill was; in fact, he left Oscar five extra dollars, even though he had a hard time getting him to accept it.

He had had a good time with the Catawba folks, and now he was on his way to a land of northern forests, beautiful crystal blue lakes and boggy wetlands. He felt more refreshed than he had in months, even with a slightly aching head from a few too many beers. He made one stop, at a small bog, where he took two ibuprofen tablets for his throbbing temples, cleaned the van carpet and caught up in his notebook. The natural beauty and wonder of the northern bog forest flooded over Garruty, and he felt the same way he'd felt on the day he'd first visited a boreal forest. He had a secret wish that he could live here, as a majestic spruce, or even a fat porcupine; then he wouldn't have to deal with all the hassles of human existence. His biophilia meter was at an all-time maximum. The mental image of his sister Rose brought him back out of the thickly interwoven evergreens. By noon he was in Eagle River.

It had been at least four years since he had seen Rose. Although she was six years older than he was, they had been close when they were growing up. She was a sweetheart who showed him how to be independent at an age when most adolescents want to be part of a group. After her teaching career ended, she married quite late in life, too late to have children. As he drove toward their lake house, he thought about her husband. Garruty didn't like Dirk. He regarded him as a lazy slacker who married his sister for her retirement money. On top of that, Dirk criticized any movement aimed at protecting the environment. I'm not getting into it with him this time, thought Garruty as he drove through the wooden gateway and down the hard-packed gravel driveway. He saw Rose kneeling in her flower garden.

"Hey Sis! How are ya?"

"Amos! Where have you been? We were expecting you earlier in the week."

"Oh, I got delayed in Illinois, and then the old van overheated. I'll tell you about it later. Gosh, it's good to see you," said Garruty as he got out of the van and gave his sister a big hug.

"Come in. Have you had lunch? I was just about to fix a sandwich. Dirk's in town."

"Sounds good. Hey, have you been crying?"

"Aw, you know I'm just an emotional woman. C'mon, I got fresh lunch meat, lettuce and tomatoes."

During lunch, Garruty told her about the trouble with the van and the folks at Oscar's Mobil station in Catawba. As he told the story, the expression on her face told him she felt uneasy. She interrupted him.

"You know, a friend of mine was from that area, and she told me about a man named Oscar. He was widely known, but I thought she said that he had passed away in the 1970s, and that the station closed shortly after that. Maybe I got it mixed up with someplace else."

Garruty changed the subject and told her the old man's story about the giant mosquito. After lunch, the brother and sister tandem went down to the pier to do a little fishing. It was a nostalgic reunion. Garruty thought about how they never just sat across from each other when they talked, they always had to be busy doing something. He baited Rose's hook with a worm, and she cast her line out just beyond the end of the pier. He looked at Rose.

"What's the matter?" he asked sincerely.

"Dirk's been going through a rough time, Ame." She had always affectionately called him Ame. She remembered how kids would tease him by calling him Amy, and how maddening it was for him because he had to hold it in. "He lost his bid for councilman, you know; on top of that his book on fly tying was rejected. Ever since that he's been really sarcastic and hard to live with."

"If he ever..."

"No, no," she quickly interrupted. "He's just been moody, he's not abusive. Look, Ame, don't you say a thing to him, it'll probably just make it worse."

Just then Rose's bobber plunged beneath the lake surface, and she gave the line a yank. Within a few seconds she pulled in a small bluegill.

"Amos, take that little fish off my hook and toss him back," she begged.

Garruty followed her orders, just as he did when they were young. As he bent over to rebait his sister's hook, Dirk silently came up from behind and blurted "Hey Bug Doctor. What ya doing, giving a bug mouth to mouth?"

"I give bugs priority over brothers-in-law in that regard," Garruty countered, then thought, Damn it, I wasn't going to fall for his digs.

"All right, Amos, touché. How was your trip?"

"Great, so far." He didn't want to talk to Dirk, and any mention of the FBI episode in Illinois would have required lengthy explanation. Besides, he didn't want Rose to know any of that either.

"Hey, did you hear the news about the strange disease outbreak?" asked Dirk.

"No, what are you talking about?"

"Oh Amos, I forgot to tell you," Rose spoke up. "They think it's a strange new virus. Looks like it first broke out in Alabama, and maybe the same thing is popping up in Illinois, somewhere, I don't remember. Several people have died."

"Is it in the paper?"

"This morning's Milwaukee Journal," she answered. Garruty got up and ran toward the house. "It's on the breakfast bar," shouted Rose.

Garruty sprang up the short steps at the back of the house and rushed through the back door, the screen door slamming behind him. He apprehensively picked up the newspaper from the breakfast bar. He couldn't believe what he read, right on the front page. Over 300 dead in northern Alabama. Thousands more there had flu-like symptoms. Doctors reported that hospitalized patients were not responding to the usual treatment for viral infections. In southern Illinois, over two hundred people were already hospitalized with rapidly alternating fever and chills, and all signs indicated that it was the same disease as the one that exploded in Alabama. Health officials announced that preliminary tests could not identify the disease agent, but they ruled out any known flu virus.

The article went on to say that most patients had complained about being bitten by mosquitoes before they got sick, but before Garruty could read that far, Rose and Dirk entered the house. They saw Garruty sitting there awestruck. He turned toward them. "I must have just missed it in Alabama and southern Illinois. I mean, I was just there, in both places where the disease popped up! One step ahead. Talk about lucky, huh?"

Rose switched on the TV and turned it to CNN. The three of them sat down and watched as an update on the disease outbreak came on. An on-the-scene correspondent reported that the number of cases in Alabama was still climbing, and the number in southern Illinois was steadily increasing. The governors of those states were declaring a state of extreme medical emergency and asking for federal aid to treat people and calling for experts to investigate the cause. The Centers for Disease Control were sending teams of epidemiologists and clinicians to both areas.

Over the next two days, the reports told of thousands of sick and dying, but what overwhelmed Garruty even more was that the disease was spreading in all directions from the two epicenters. Judging by the rate at which it was spreading, experts suspected that the disease agent had become airborne. Garruty, Rose and Dirk talked about how far the virus would spread, and whether it could be contained at all.

The next morning, Garruty threw his bag in the van and turned to say good-bye to Rose and Dirk. "I hate that we couldn't fish for crappies yesterday. I think it would have been a banner day for them," Dirk piped up. Dusk was the time they usually had the most luck catching crappies, but late June was also the time mosquitoes came out in hordes.

"Hey, next time. Maybe I'll come back by after I spend some time in the U.P.," Garruty answered.

Rose smiled and said, "We'll be looking forward to it Ame. Take care, little brother. I love you." Garruty was sure she knew he wouldn't be back for a long time.

Garruty gave her a long hug and then shook hands with Dirk. During the last several days he and Dirk had partially closed the rift between them, and Garruty felt better about their relationship and about his sister being married to Dirk. When he got in the van he rolled down the window and yelled, "Wave to the corner!"

In less than half an hour, Garruty was in the Upper Peninsula of Michigan. "Oh yeah, the U.P." he exclaimed. "The land of rivers, lakes, bogs, and Somatochlora, that group of rare, metallic green northern dragonflies that all dragonfly aficionados go ape over! Been way too long since I was here."

He drove north to Watersmeet, then headed east at a slow pace, taking small roads so he could see as much natural scenery as possible. Going north, he stopped at Pictured Rocks National Lakeshore, a natural wonder with mineral-stained sandstone cliffs, sculpted by wind, ice and pounding waves and colored in shades of brown, tan, and green, rising 200 feet above Lake Superior in places. Thinking the mosquitoes wouldn't be as bad there as further inland, he took a chance at getting a campsite in the backcountry campgrounds and it paid off. He had a restful evening, the first in several months. The next day he made his way toward the Straits of Mackinac, and then continued along the northern shore of Lake Huron, reaching his destination of Cedarville by mid afternoon.

The lakeshore near Cedarville was clean, as if the pebbles and sand had been carefully washed; the smells of a variety of evergreens weighed heavy in the air. "Ah," Garruty sighed, "Gitchee Gumee at last."

It was a rather still day, and the cool crystal-clear water was gently splashing up against some isolated huge boulders not far from Garruty's campsite. Just before sundown he lit a small fire with the dry wood he'd found earlier and fixed his campsite version of au gratin potatoes in aluminum foil. The smoke drifted upward and filled his nostrils, and at times invaded his eyes and made them sting. In the dimming twilight, he wrote about his latest experiences in his personal journal. At dusk he slowly toasted some marshmallows over the red, ebbing coals.

Feeling rested, and again in the absence of pesky mosquitoes, he decided to stay up late and walk along the dimly lit shore. The quarter moon reflected off the tops of the gentle waves. The cool water invigorated his toes, and he waded in up to his knees. He thought about the legend of the giant mosquito, and the town of Cheboygan, the supposed site of the Great Mosquito Festival; tomorrow he would see if the legend was still celebrated.

As he waded along the shore, the sliver of moon now below its zenith, he saw the reflection of a firefly in the dark water.

"Hello, Longfellow's little Wah-wah-taysee," whispered Garruty.

Soon there were dozens, and then hundreds, but when he looked up, to his bewilderment, he saw not one. He looked down into the water and saw them again. Looking up, again there was not one in the air. Surreal as it seemed, he had to believe that they were "flying" around in the water. He leaned downward, straining his eyes close to the water's surface. The fireflies, now numbering thousands, circled and made a great swirl of light. Mesmerized, he was drawn closer until his face plunged into the water. Suddenly the swirl created a whirlpool and he was drawn in, headfirst. In a flash he was swirled around the Les Cheneaux Islands, then downward, until he was sucked down to the bottom of Lake Huron. He felt as though he were outside his body. By the light of the fireflies, he caught sight of a sunken cabin boat and swam toward it for all he was worth. Guided now by the dim light cast from the cabin door, Garruty pounded his fists on the rugged exterior, his lungs burning and about to take in water. Within seconds a gaunt man appeared, looked out the small round window, and slid the door open. Garruty was instantly washed into the boat, after which the door quickly snapped shut. The man led Garruty through another door into the interior cabin.

"How did you get here, and who are you?" exclaimed the man.

"I was walking along the lakeshore, when I saw these fireflies, and..."

"So, you know about the fireflies," interrupted the man. "What's your name?"

"Amos Garruty. What's yours?"

"Garruty. Garruty. I know that name from somewhere." He paused. "I'm Porter Hutson. Hey, are you OK?"

"Yes, but I could use a towel," he said, shivering.

Then Garruty realized what the man had said and blurted out, "Porter Hutson? The Porter Hutson that the legend of Hutsonwatha is based on? Man, that was some tale."

Small, piercing black eyes peered over the rims of narrow, wire-framed glasses, squinting and staring at Garruty as if he had called him an outright liar. "Tale huh? Let me tell you something, that was no tale! It happened just like in the poem," he snapped.

"Look, sorry. I, uh, it just seems that no one out there takes it seriously."

"I know. What do think I'm doing down here? I couldn't take the doubt and sarcasm anymore."

"How the hell do you live down here?" asked Garruty.

"Quite well, thank you. Well, I have to admit, every once in a while I go up and sneak in supplies. I've got a small generator to provide power, but except for the air system, I don't need much power. As far as keeping busy, I study the lake bottom fauna, as much as I want. My life-long goal. I just don't have contact with people anymore, and I don't miss it."

Garruty looked around the small quarters. The cabin looked somewhat like the inside of a submarine, all joints heavily reinforced and double sealed. The walls were of a beautiful, smooth-grained hardwood, stained dark red. Countless books and scientific papers were stacked just below the level of the small oval windows. Except for the low ceiling, the place looked comfortable. Garruty figured the floor was raised, as they weren't standing in water.

Garruty turned and asked Hutson point blank, "How do I know what you claim about the giant mosquito is true?"

Hutson showed Garruty a huge ugly scar between two of his ribs just to the right of his sternum, claiming that was where the giant mosquito's proboscis punctured his chest. He also had a picture of himself with one of the mosquito's giant wings that he had carried back. Garruty was convinced. He had always been fascinated by the legend and wanted to believe it was true; now he had evidence. The two old entomologists talked for over an hour, forming a bond. Hutson explained that after the battle with the giant mosquito, which occurred over 40 years ago, certain influential people didn't believe his story and they tried to discredit him. Things got pretty ugly. So, frustrated and embarrassed, he disappeared. At that, Garruty wasn't sure about going down to Cheboygan, as there probably wasn't a celebration at all. And he was beginning to feel that avoiding crowds right now might be best for him.

"I sure would like to spend more time here, Hutsonwatha, but my research...um, I'm getting behind schedule; I need to get back. Is that possible?" asked Garruty.

"Oh yes. Just go with the fireflies. It's not very far. Before you know it, you'll be back on the lakeshore."

The next morning Garruty woke up on the lakeshore, sprawled out on a wet towel with sand stuck all over his body. He sat up and tried to brush it off. Still feeling gritty and sticky, he stripped and dove into the lake. Drying off in the van, he thought about his new friend at the bottom of the lake. "A hero, and now exiled," he mumbled, then thought about the old man. Poor Hutson. There he is, carrying on his work alone; he might as well be on another planet. No contact with others. Geez, he'll never publish all that data on the bottom fauna of the Great Lakes, no matter how much new information he finds. Why is he doing all that work? Then the answer, the only answer, dawned on him—what else would he do?

Garruty had some fruit for breakfast. While eating he anxiously turned on the radio, hoping to catch up on the news. He tuned in to NPR, and despite the bad reception, he soon heard that the epidemic in Alabama and Illinois was worsening and that it had recently popped up in north central Wisconsin.

Wait a minute, thought Garruty. It started at home, now it's shown up nearly everywhere I stopped on my trip north. And in all those places, mosquitoes bit the hell out of me.

A chill came over him at his next thought. When I went back in time, I got bit a lot, then I got sick with the same symptoms that they're reporting. Did I bring it back from some ancient past? No, I'd be sick too.

His thoughts were interrupted by a special report announcing that the FBI and CDC were conducting a manhunt. In between bouts of static he heard parts of an interview with Agent Booker, now recovered, who mentioned Garruty's name. He cried out, "Oh my God, they're looking for me"!

Knowing he had to keep from panicking, Garruty quickly came up with a plan. He bought a local newspaper and in the Want Ads section found an ad placed by a man who wanted to buy a used van. Garruty drove out to Big Trout Lake to see him, and when he found out the man wanted to see the great American West, he sold him his van.

"Is there any way I can hitch a boat ride over to the North Channel?" Garruty asked.

"I have a friend who has a 20-footer, and I think he makes that trip just about every week in the summer. I can give him a call, if you want."

"Yes, please. I'll make it worth his while if he'll let me ride along."

Within a few minutes the man returned. "Well, you're in luck. He's leaving for Little Current day after tomorrow. Said he's got plenty of room if you want to go along. All you got to do is meet him Friday, 7 a.m. at St. Vital Point."

"Thanks, thanks a lot. Is there anywhere close by that I can camp until Friday?"

"There's a campground at De Tour State Park, just a few miles from here. Hey, I can give you a ride in my new used van!"

Garruty took advantage of the extra day to catch up in his notebooks. Friday morning came fast. He walked down to the point and at 7:00 sharp met Shipper Truman, who owned The Lacewing, a 20-foot inboard.

Shipper practically lived on the Great Lakes. He was a retired naval officer from Buffalo, now turned aquatic adventurer. Garruty transferred the belongings and supplies that he anticipated needing to the boat. His load was getting lighter, as he left behind the perishable goods and most of his camping equipment. He met the other shipmates, Wheezer and Ray Solong, two brothers with just two interests, birding and drinking. Before long they were motoring eastward along the shore of Lake Huron, heading right for the Canadian border.

This ought to make it harder for them to trace me, he thought. But I feel like a fugitive.

YANKEE STADIUM
ephone

6

Caterpillars in the Big Apple

The boat ride east to Drummond Island got choppier as the morning wind picked up. The sudden, regular slapping of the boat against the waves jarred Garruty's frangible bones. It felt like his jaw was becoming detached. He was relieved to finally see the passageway to the North Channel. Here the surface was much calmer, the clear water protected from the wind by the mass of the islands and their cover of pine, spruce, fir and hemlock. As they skirted the north shore of Manitoulin Island, his nervous state began to ebb, slowly calming like the water's surface. Now in Canadian waters, he felt a bit more secure. Gazing through binoculars into the shallower, smaller embayments, he saw many kinds of water birds, including numerous cormorants and several kinds of gulls. Shipper carefully maneuvered in and out of several of the weedier coves so they could get closer looks at the wildlife. Suddenly Garruty's eyes felt like they were being pulled through the lenses. Standing a few inches from the edge of the water was a medium-sized, mostly white gull.

"Gee whiz, that's got to be a Black-legged Kittiwake," he yelled.

Wheezer came over and snatched the glasses from Garruty's grasp. "Can't be. Where?" he snapped.

Struggling without aid of the binoculars, Garruty pointed toward a clump of emergent weeds, and said, "Over there, to the right of those weeds."

Wheezer finally caught a glimpse of the bird as it disappeared over the trees. "Naw, had to be some other gull. You'd never see a Kittiwake this far inland, especially not in June."

Garruty disliked someone doubting him. He persisted, "What other gull has a yellow bill and solid black wing tips? I got a good look at it."

"Herring gulls are fairly common here," added Wheezer's brother. Ray wasn't looking through his binoculars, as he was too occupied keeping his glass of scotch from spilling.

"But I saw the legs, you guys, they were black."

Shipper interrupted, "OK guys, let's cool it. Maybe we'll see it again."

Garruty held out little hope of that.

It was late afternoon by the time they pulled into Gore Bay, swerved around sailboats of all sizes and eased up to the pier. "Thanks, and good luck on the rest of your voyage," Garruty said as he gave Shipper the $100 he promised.

"Good luck to you too, mate," came the reply.

Garruty stepped onto the wooden pier with his gear, wobbling a bit at first. He saw that the pier, ropes, telephone wires and surrounding trees were ornamented with countless hanging mayflies, those fragile long-tailed gossamers that dwell in the soft lake bottom for a year and then emerge synchronously by the millions. Willow flies to Alabamians, he thought. He knew that at dusk these short-lived adults would take to the air and form huge mating swarms; then in the dark of night each female would flop into the water and release thousands of eggs as her life waned. It was smorgasbord time for fish. Suddenly the smell of food, especially the aroma of sautéed onions and green peppers coming from the nearby restaurant, was a piercing reminder of how hungry he'd gotten. He quietly stepped inside and looked around. Passing the "Seat Yourself" sign, he saw that the dining room was full. As he approached a small table, the only one with an empty seat, a lady sitting there asked him to sit down.

"Oh, I wouldn't want to intrude," he replied.

"No, please sit. Look around. There's no other seat, and I could sure use some conversation."

Jenine was from Montreal and was on a three-week vacation. Her short blond hair was slightly wavy, and she had black eyes, a turned-up nose and pouty lips. Garruty thought she might be in her late thirties.

"What's your name?" she asked.

Thinking for a few seconds, he answered, "Pete," and then paused. "Pete um...Malone." He wasn't giving up his true identity to anyone at this point.

"Well, hi Pete-Pete," she giggled. "Can I call you RePete?"

After this awkward introduction, they talked about their travels and began to tell each other a little about themselves. Suddenly the door burst open and in sprang a person dressed in a flimsy, colorful mayfly costume, long tails and all. It flapped its wings and hopped through the crowded restaurant in mock flight, knocking some jars of jelly to the floor, singing Eee-yay-wy, revere the mayfly! The owner rushed out from the kitchen and hit the goofy-looking mayfly over the head with a large frying pan, knocking it to the floor. Several of the busboys dragged the "mayfly" out of the dining room and left it lying in a dazed heap on the pier.

"Danged bugs," snapped the owner as he went back to the kitchen.

Garruty and Jenine looked at each other and broke into laughter. They continued talking, and before long their food was served. It was one of the most enjoyable dinner engagements Garruty had had in years, and he realized he was becoming fond of her. As they finished eating, she asked if he was staying in the area.

"Well, I hope so," he said, "but I just got here, and I haven't tried to get a room yet."

"Well, I checked earlier today, and there are no vacancies anywhere around here this weekend. Say, if you can't find anything, there are a couple of open campsites on the island I'm camping on. You're welcome there, that is if you like to camp."

Garruty felt reluctant initially, but then he realized it was getting late and he probably had no other choice. "I don't have a boat; are there any for rent around here?"

"Don't worry about that, I can give you a ride."

"Yeah? Are you sure?"

"Yes, c'mon. We better get going."

When Jenine stood up, Garruty immediately noticed her stature. Gosh, she's really short, maybe five foot three. He found himself sizing her up without really thinking. Never in his whole life had he been attracted to short women. As much as he liked her, especially her personality, he decided to keep things platonic.

As Jenine's boat parted the water toward Chippewa Island, they couldn't keep their eyes away from the western horizon. The setting sun was painting a dazzling purple and orange mural below a twisted mass of dark, cheese curl clouds. Garruty sat there imagining that the bottoms of the clouds were massive floating, slow-burning coals.

As they pulled into the island's small embayment, Jenine exclaimed that she had never seen more beautiful sunsets than those in the North Channel. Although Garruty had seen spectacular sunsets all around the world, he politely agreed with her.

"This is like a dream," he said.

They tied up the boat and Garruty unloaded the things he would need for the night. The island was a huge, uninhabited granite outcrop that was largely covered with white pine trees. Jenine had found a level open area blanketed with a bed of pine needles. He set up his small pup tent about 30 feet from hers. As he was tying it down, Jenine came over.

"Want a small glass of Merlot?"

"I don't drink wine very often, but that sounds good. Thanks. Say, there's a nice log back here that we can sit on. I'll start a fire; wanna talk for awhile?"

"Sounds good," she answered.

The bright stars filtering through the tall aromatic pines provided a rare romantic island setting. But Garruty wasn't feeling romantic. When he told her that he had worked on insects as a career, Jenine remembered the morning news updating the disease outbreak. She told him that the number of people dead was nearing a thousand, as the strange, unprecedented disease continued spreading throughout the south central states and the upper Midwest. Even clinicians, nurses and doctors were getting sick, and health officials feared that the virus-like agent had mutated and become infectious by contact. There was a long silence.

Jenine changed the subject and told him she had only three days of vacation left and then she would have to go back to her job in architectural design. He told her that he definitely wasn't heading back to the Midwest. Instead he was thinking about going to New York, but he didn't say anything about his ex-wife. When he looked at her full lips in the glow of the fire, he felt a yearning deep inside that he hadn't felt in over a decade. He turned his gaze to the fire and forced himself to suppress his feelings. They talked a while longer, but she sensed he was getting pretty tired. As the crackling of their small fire died down, they said good night and retired to their tents.

Tired as he was, Garruty felt uneasy inside the small tent. After an hour of lying on his back and obsessing over all the things going on, he quietly went out and laid his foam rubber mattress and sleeping bag on the thick pine straw. He sat on his bedroll and looked up into the black, star-studded sky. The basic questions of life passed through his mind: who am I; what am I doing; where am I going? He put his face in his hands; no answers came, not that he expected any. He changed his posture to the perfect position. He slowly and methodically performed a few of his favorite yoga exercises, ending with lying flat on his back, trying to relax totally and empty his mind of all thought. With his eyes closed, he began to feel weightless, as if he were being elevated to the tops of the pines. Garruty now began to see things more clearly. I can't have the virus, or I'd be sick. But if I do have it, especially if it can be transmitted by contact, Jenine could get it. As much as he was falling for her, he had to refrain from getting too close.

He wondered if Jenine had fallen asleep. She must be wondering why I am so elusive. It seems like she dropped a few hints that she was interested in me. I know I'm not good at reading people's minds, especially women's. Even if she was interested, I'm too old for her. And she's too short for me.

Garruty woke up to the soft patter of raindrops on his face. He got up and moved his bedding inside his tent. His shuffling woke Jenine, and she sat up.

"Hey Pete, were you sleeping outside?" she asked through the netting.

"It was such a beautiful evening, I couldn't resist. It's not raining hard now, but it looks like it's getting darker. I think we ought to head back to Gore Bay. What do you think?"

"The way these rainy systems can hang in for days, and this feels like one of those, I think you're right."

The heavy mist over the channel made the boat ride back to the harbor of Gore Bay a wet one. Garruty was glad he had packed his notebooks in heavy plastic bags. Once they reached the bay, Jenine left her friend's boat in a nearby boathouse. They inquired in the restaurant if there were any rooms available in Gore City, as the folks there were sure to be aware of the current situation in the area. The owner called several places and found that all rooms were reserved, so they loaded their gear in Jenine's SUV and headed east. Fortunately they found two vacancies at Wikikong's Bed & Breakfast, near Killarney Provincial Park. They spent most of the day walking, talking and window-shopping at several antique shops.

The next day started out partly cloudy, so they made the short drive to the Killarney to hike the spectacular white quartzite ridges and experience the wilderness of the most majestic park in eastern Canada. When they parked the SUV, the clouds were vanishing and the sun was becoming intense, so they left the windows slightly open. As they casually hiked the sandy crevices between the ridges, the only sights spoiling the scenery were the frequent heavy infestations of large tent caterpillars on the hardwood trees, especially on the black cherries. The caterpillars were actually quite pretty, gray and black with tufts of long red hairs on top. Garruty told her to ignore the damage they did and instead look at the white granite outcrops; he told her they were the marshmallows that God left behind for the giant unicorns. As they stood side by side on top of one of the outcrops, thrilled by their view of the park, she turned to him, put her arms around his waist, and reached up to kiss him. His put his forefinger over her lips, then pulled away.

"I'm sorry, Jenine, I can't." He couldn't remember a more awkward moment in his entire life.

They continued hiking the trail in silence. Jenine refrained from asking what was wrong. Garruty felt bad that he couldn't explain his worries to her, and he was sorry he had hurt her feelings by ending the moment. When they approached the next high, rounded ridge, they stopped abruptly. There in broad daylight, at the flat top of the ridge, was a large group of people, all stark naked, holding hands and slowly moving in a circle. They were wearing large masks that were shaped like the head of a mosquito with a long beak, and they were chanting something about mosquitoes bringing about the end of the world, and that the time was now. The two hikers watched for a short time as the group changed the direction of the circle back and forth. They decided to turn around and head back.

While they had been away from the vehicle, hundreds of moths had flown inside through the openings in the windows and concealed themselves underneath the seats, carpet, and inside the spare tire well. The moths were about an inch long, dark brown, and their forewings had a red mark shaped like a skull and crossbones. The stout proboscis was black. Garruty and Jenine drove back to Wikikong's Bed and Breakfast, agreeing not to see each other that evening.

The next morning, the long drive to Montreal was mostly silent. About half way there, she asked him to drive, as she wasn't feeling well. When they pulled into town, she complained of a headache and said she thought she had a fever. Garruty helped her inside her apartment and took care of her the rest of the day, hoping it wasn't what he thought. Her fever got worse, and that evening when it switched to chills, he quickly took her to the hospital. That evening she had hallucinations and was somewhat incoherent. Garruty held her hand and thought, she better not die!

In the middle of the night, she woke up and whispered, "I wish you had fallen for me the way I did for you." Tears came to his eyes.

The next morning, she woke to find Garruty asleep in the chair by her bed. "Hey, how long have you been there?"

"Since last night. How are you?"

"I feel better, but weak."

He told her his fears, that although he didn't think he was responsible for the disease outbreak, he just wasn't sure, and that was the reason he didn't want to get close to her. "You're not sick, you can't have it. And see, I'm feeling better already."

Later that day, Garruty told her he wanted to go to New York, to see his ex-wife, but he wasn't sure how he was going to get there. She told him to take her old SUV, as she was planning to buy a new one anyway. He offered to pay her for it, but she said, "Just come back and see me someday, OK?"

After a long good-bye, Garruty got in the SUV and sped for New York with a heavy heart. He felt he had left one of the most delightful and lovable people he had ever met. "Damn it, I can't be carrying the germ. I'd be sick," he cursed under his breath. He propped Jenine's picture up on the dashboard, looking at it periodically.

Suddenly he felt something tickling his ankle. He took his foot off the accelerator and spied a moth fluttering up his leg; all of a sudden he felt a sharp prick on the inner part of his calf. He swatted the moth and threw it out.

"That thing couldn't have bitten me! Moths don't bite!" he exclaimed.

Deep in thought, he drove into New York City. There was no reason to believe the deadly microbe wouldn't move east. I can't change anything now, but if I am carrying the virus, maybe I can stop it from getting worse. If the virologists can diagnose this germ and come up with a vaccine or something... But if I turn myself in, I don't know what they'll do to me.

It was then that Garruty realized he better not go to see Adele. He couldn't stand the thought of her contracting the disease. He became determined not to have physical contact with anyone. He drove aimlessly through the Bronx until he saw Yankee Stadium. There has to be a public phone booth around here. At least I can call her and see how she's doing, and warn her about the disease.

He found an unoccupied phone booth and searched through his wallet for Adele's phone number. As he thumbed through the small pieces of paper on which he had written personal phone numbers, he came across his sister's number first. "Rose!" he exclaimed. Gosh, I wonder if she's all right, he thought and decided to call her first. He found a small piece of plastic to wrap around the phone and dialed. It seemed like the phone rang a very long time. Finally Rose answered. She told him that she had gotten very sick but recovered, but Dirk succumbed to the virus, as did several other local people. He called Adele next. She was surprised to hear his voice, but glad to know he was all right. She had been keeping up on the spread of the virus, and asked how he had avoided getting it. Then she remembered something.

"Amos, some federal agents were here, and they wanted to know your whereabouts. They're thinking you'll show up here sooner or later."

Garruty thought, I am being targeted! Before she could finish telling him what Agent Booker said, he wished her well and hung up. While he was on the phone, Garruty had a full view of the SUV. The moths had become active while he talked and they had gathered at the top of the window he had left slightly open. He watched them continuously stream out of the SUV and into Yankee Stadium. He wondered, What the heck? Where did they come from? How did so many get in the SUV?

Garruty was startled by a sharp knock on the phone booth glass. A chiseled man with black, slicked back hair, black eyes and a black suit was motioning for him to get off the phone. Although Garruty was about to hang up the receiver anyway, he resented the man's rude manners. He opened the door, stepped out and started to give the man a dirty look. When their eyes met, Garruty was instantly intimidated; he had never seen a more icy, menacing look. The man put his left hand on Garruty's face and cursing, pushed him up against the booth.

"Just open your mouth," he growled. When Garruty just stood there trembling, he ordered, "Aw, get outa here, ya coward."

Garruty put his head down and turned toward the SUV, walking away slowly. For the first time in his life, he had a realistic anticipation of what it would feel like to get a knife in the back. When he reached his vehicle, the only sound he heard was his heart beating. He walked around to the passenger side, unlocked the door and sat down. After a few minutes his adrenalin subsided and he peeked over toward the booth without turning his head; the intimidator was looking toward the SUV, but he had the phone to his ear.

Garruty sat there a while longer, shifting his thoughts back to the moths. He checked all over the inside of the SUV but didn't see any more hiding. He looked up at the mammoth stadium. There was no baseball that day, just some people gathering to go on tour groups. He figured there wasn't any way he could stop the moths now, and besides, what harm could the little hitchhikers do? To the contrary, he felt a little sad for them, as they were sure to starve to death in this "concrete jungle".

During this thoughtful moment, he didn't realize that his blank stare had been directed toward the phone booth. His near stupor was interrupted by a sudden commotion. Several policemen, two under-cover agents and a man wearing an FBI jacket were running toward the booth. They ordered the man who had confronted Garruty out of the booth and quickly handcuffed and searched him. They must think he's me, Garruty thought. He slid over to the driver's side of the SUV and did his best impression of Dale Earnheardt.

Because Garruty didn't know anyone else in the city and he liked New York now even less than before, he decided to drive south to Philadelphia. He remembered that his friend and colleague there, Dr. Sam Roe, once told him to stop by anytime he was in the area. As he left the city, he saw advertisements for the upcoming three-game series between the Yankees and the Boston Red Sox. The signs read, "Yankees Back In Town Friday. Mission: SWEEP THE RED SOX. GO WHITEY AND MICKY." He hadn't kept up with baseball for two decades, ever since it seemed more like a business than a game.

"No loyalty anymore; it's all about the money," he lamented. "Besides, the Yankees win all the time."

En route to Philadelphia, Garruty realized he was making a grave mistake. If I go see Sam, I'll just take all my troubles to him. And I can't take the risk of putting any more of my friends in danger. I'll just hide out for a few days until this thing dies down. Sure about that one thing, but unsure about most everything else, he headed for the Pine Barrens of New Jersey.

Chatsworth wasn't what Garruty thought. It was small, so small there were no motels. Tired and stiff, he stopped at an antique shop, which seemed to be all there was in this quaint village. The little shop looked full and empty at the same time—full of junk, empty of people.

"Anyone here?" he called out.

"Just a minute, be right with you," came a voice from a back room.

He could hear shoes shuffling across an uneven wooden floor. After a minute, a bent-over little lady shuffled through the narrow doorway and sat down on a stool behind the counter. She slowly looked up at Garruty. "Sorry, how can I help you?"

"Hello Ma'am. Is there any way to get a room for the night around here?" He kept a considerable distance from the counter.

She wrinkled the dry skin around her beady eyes and in her scratchy voice snapped, "I ain't no ma'am, and no, there ain't no motels here. There is a campground just a few miles east."

"Mosquitoes..."

"Bad, real bad," she interrupted.

Garruty let out a sigh; he looked exasperated. She slowly slid off the stool and leaning forward rested her arms on top of the counter. Her expression became a little warmer.

"Listen, my son-in-law has a shack outside of town that he sometimes rents out. It ain't much, but I can call him if you're interested."

"I am, ma... uh..."

"Sadie," she filled in for him. "Even the kids around here call me Sadie."

"OK, Sadie. Sorry. Yes, I really need someplace to, er, rest."

At 3:30, Garruty met Stan Hawkins near Chatsworth Lake Dam, just as Sadie arranged. Stan got out of his truck and spit tobacco juice on the ground. Garruty wasn't sure if there was more dark stuff on the ground or on his monstrous mustache. Garruty introduced himself, but kept his distance and did not extend his hand. They went inside and Garruty took a quick look around.

"How long you want her for, a month?"

"I don't need it that long, can I just have it for a week," asked Garruty.

"Yeah, I guess so. That'll be $170, up front."

"OK, but I'll have to go back and get some cash. Is there an ATM in town?"

"Yeah, I guess so," Stan replied, although his expression told Garruty he really didn't know what an ATM was.

When Garruty got back to the shack, he was glad he had held onto his bedroll all this time. Except for a few wooden chairs, a warped table, a tumbledown old easy chair and the countless spider webs, the two-room shack was nearly bare. At least there was an old bed in the tiny bedroom, even though the box spring sagged. It wasn't what he would have preferred, but at this point in time, the location was perfect. He spent the next few days traversing the lake edge, nearby swamps and waterways, and making observations on all types of insects; he filled numerous pages in his field book with detailed notes. Each day, by late afternoon, the mosquito hordes chased him back to the shack. Though the shack was in need of paint and structural upkeep, he was thankful that the window screens were intact.

By Saturday, Garruty was in need of provisions. He had brought very little food with him, and he was getting tired of wild berries. He also felt a growing hot itch all over his legs and suspected he had gotten into some poison ivy. He knew he'd better get it treated, so he put his notebooks in his backpack and threw it and a few other necessities in the SUV. There was no medical clinic in Chatsworth, so in his desperate state he headed for the outskirts of Philadelphia.

In the waiting room of the first medical clinic he found, he picked up the Saturday edition of the New York Times. His jaw dropped when he read the front-page headline: "Yankee Stadium Collapses, Hundreds Killed". He read on. During the seventh inning stretch of the Friday night game between the Yankees and the Red Sox, countless large brown moths flew all over the stadium, biting people and driving everybody to panic. The commotion created tremendous stress on the old stadium and it collapsed, crushing thousands of fans. The Yankees' dugout, which was on the first base side of the field, was crushed by a huge sliding piece of the upper deck. Some of the Bronx Bombers and coaches were killed and many others were seriously injured.

Garruty was stunned, and a numbing feeling in his brain, as if his head were swelling, came over him. His eyes drifted down the page. At the bottom was another report that caught his attention. "CDC Identifies Deadly Virus." The article said that the agent of the deadly new disease had been identified as a virus with a very different structure than any known; some virologists speculated that it was a primitive virus. They were now sure that it had mutated to a highly virulent strain, and was being spread via contact; they indicated that it was not an airborne pathogen. Large parts of Alabama, Tennessee, Kentucky, Illinois and Wisconsin had been infected and it was moving in an eastward direction. It was estimated that two to three weeks after appearing in an area, the death rate could climb to 40%!

"Mr. Garruty," came a voice through the waiting room. There was a pause. "Mr. Garruty? Is there a Mr. Garruty here?"

At the third mention of his name, he realized he had given them his real name. He got up, put the newspaper down and walked toward the attendant holding the door open for him. He was led to a private room and told to sit in the chair. After the nurse took his vital signs, she told him to lie down on the examination table and began to examine the rash on his legs, which by now had developed numerous blisters, some of which were oozing a clear fluid. During this time, a doctor came into the room, read his chart and then quickly left.

"We're going to have to wash your legs and then we'll apply some medicine for you. Dr. Haskill will be in to see you shortly. The doctor may also prescribe an oral corticosteroid if the itching doesn't subside soon."

After a few minutes, a clinician entered the room, treated his legs and then left. "The doctor will be in soon," she told him.

Shortly the lotion began to sooth his itchy skin. Garruty rested prone in the examination room for over 10 minutes before the door opened again. The doctor entered, followed by two other men, a tall man wearing a black suit, the other a diminutive fellow wearing gray slacks and a light blue shirt and tie.

Garruty was surprised to see the doctor sit and the man dressed in black approach him first.

"So. Dr. Garruty, you're a pretty elusive fellow. We've been wanting to talk to you."

"What's the matter?"

"We're hoping you'll tell us. We need to know where you've been and what you've been doing. Are you aware of the epidemic throughout the Midwest, and how it's spreading eastward?"

Garruty felt an adrenaline rush but remained silent. He was doing some quick thinking.

"And you better tell us where you got that SUV."

After a few seconds, Garruty responded, "I have pocket lint, 'n..." He paused, sat up and bent over as if to scratch his legs. "Ooh, ouch; Doctor, my legs," he groaned. When Dr. Haskill got up to examine him, he spun and pushed him into the tall man. Garruty clumsily bolted through the door, right into the arms of two policemen. They escorted him back into the examination room and pushed him back onto the cold table.

The scrawny psychiatrist spoke up. "Let me ask a few questions, Stricker." To Garruty this guy looked like the demonic little torturer in a horror movie. In a nasal voice he asked, "Mr. Garruty, did you know that people have been dying wherever you go?"

Garruty didn't answer.

"Have you thought about that? Does that mean anything to you?"

"Bibbidy-bobbidy-boo," slurred Garruty, but then fell silent again. His eyes looked glazed. Because he had eaten only a few blueberries and raspberries in the last three days, he was extremely weak. His allergic reaction to the urushiol, the irritating oil in poison ivy, was worsening. He felt faint and was losing his equilibrium; he started to drool. When he mumbled a few words about moths biting him in the legs, and hitchhikers in the SUV, the doctor intervened. "We need to get this man to a hospital," he said angrily.

At that point, Garruty started to fall off the examination table, but they caught him and put him on a stretcher. Dr. Haskill ordered an IV for him and then emphatically recommended he be sent to Atlanta to be treated by a colleague of his, a specialist in mental trauma. Everyone agreed that would be best, as they certainly weren't going to learn anything from him in this state. He was still unconscious when they arrived at the airport. As they began to unload him from the ambulance, Garruty regained consciousness and tried to get up from the stretcher. Losing his balance, he lurched forward and fell into an anchored waste receptacle; his head struck heavily against the metal side, knocking him unconscious again.

7

Holy Mantis

Still stumbling in the fuzzy darkness behind his eyelids, Garruty felt something tickling his neck. He also sensed warm air, like a soft breath, brush his cheek and eyelashes, and he realized that someone was very close to him. He opened his eyes, not knowing where he was. As the white-clad clinician leaned over him to adjust his IV, he tried to focus his vision and asked weakly, "Are you an angel?"

"No," came the answer with a giggle. She moved back a little.

Without his glasses on, she looked out-of-focus, but he could tell she was attractive. "I never imagined (pause), a terminal angel would be (pause), so pretty," he added.

"I'm not an angel, certainly not a terminal one!" she replied.

He tried to look into her soft brown eyes, but she immediately avoided direct contact with his steely blue eyes.

"I guess that's good. Oh God, my head hurts," he said, as he tried to reach up to feel his forehead. He realized his arms and torso were strapped to the bed.

"Well, I'm not surprised Dr. Garruty. You hit that garbage can pretty hard."

"I, I don't remember. Why am I being constrained?"

Surprised at his alertness, she answered him politely. "Your chart said you were very disturbed, possibly dangerous. The doctors ordered the restraints mainly to protect you."

"How did you know my name?"

"It's on your chart. And, well, I have to admit, I glanced at some of your notebooks. You..."

"My notebooks! Where are they? And where am I?"

She told him what happened in Philadelphia and that a few of his belongings, such as his backpack, were sent with him when he was transported to the ward in Atlanta.

"I hope you're telling me the truth. What's your name?" he asked.

"Look, we're not supposed to socialize with the patients." After a brief pause, she added, "But I guess it won't hurt to tell you. I'm Ms. Ortiz."

Carmela Ortiz was in her early 40s; she was about 5' 7" tall and weighed 122 lbs. Her brown eyes had a luster he had never seen in anyone's eyes before. She had very long, slightly curly, dark brown hair and a perfect figure. Her skin was smooth and had a lightly tanned look indicative of her Hispanic and Italian descent. He found her Spanish accent especially charming, but she seemed very business-like.

"My friends call me Pancake." She turned to leave and he pleaded, "My arms hurt, can you undo these straps?"

"I'm not authorized to do that, sorry."

Garruty's next words stopped her cold. "I thought I had died. That was unsettling, but being tied down like this, I don't know which is worse. I'm claustrophobic enough without being confined. How do think you would feel?"

She hesitated and then turned. "Um, maybe I can..."

Just then a heavy-set nurse stepped into the room. "Well, well, look who's awake," she cracked. "How we feeling?"

"We," replied Garruty, emphasizing the pronoun, "would like to be left alone."

"Oh, that right? What's going on in here, Carmela?"

"Nothing. I'll try to find that magazine you wanted, sir," she said and briskly left the room.

Garruty caught Carmela's ruse about the magazine. He closed his eyes and started humming the tune to "Fat Bottomed Girls You Make The Rocking World Go Round." As the nurse tended to her tasks, he did his best to ignore her. He had just met the most beautiful woman he'd ever seen and he didn't want anyone breaking up his mental image of her. He hoped she would return. Then he began to remember the mess he was in and worried, What if I'm a carrier?

Garruty suffered through the rest of that day and the next. The only time the straps around him were loosened was when he had to roll over to use the bedpan; he was kept under constant guard. The most frustrating thing was that he hadn't yet been able to see a way out of there. Also, there was no Carmela during this time, which might have been a bigger disappointment. He began to wonder if he made her up, but her smell lingered almost as real as life; if she did exist, he suspected that she had been transferred from his care. Several analysts came in to ask questions. Instead of speaking to them, he made strange chirping sounds like a cricket. When they got frustrated and began to leave, he would chant in a high-pitched voice, "Vanilla ice cream with Carmela sauce, please."

The next morning, he woke up to a sweet voice softly calling his name. "Dr. Garruty. Dr. Garruty, please wake up." He opened his eyes and there she was, sitting next to his bed. "How are you doing?" Carmela asked.

"Ms. Ortiz; not so good. I asked to see you, but no one would tell me if you were coming back. I thought perhaps you had been ordered not to see me."

"No, I was away for a couple days. I see you're still strapped down."

"Yes. I haven't been very cooperative. Some creeps keep coming in, asking me questions about where I've been and what I've been doing. I need to get out of here before they terminate me."

"What?" she gasped.

"I'm sure they think that I brought the virus back from the ancient past."

She looked puzzled.

"You know—the one that is creating the epidemic? Look, they've been taking blood samples from me constantly, and they even did a spinal tap. They've analyzed me enough to get what they need, I'm sure of it, and any moment now they're going to end it. The next injection could be a lethal one. You've got to help me get out of here!"

"Please, Dr. Garruty, shhhh; calm down. You want me to believe you're not crazy, well this sounds pretty crazy, you know. How do I know what you say is true?"

"My notebooks. I've kept a journal of everything that's happened this summer. You said you read a little bit before. Just read through this summer's journal, it's all there, you'll see; but do it quickly."

"I don't see your backpack anywhere."

"Oh no, they've got my journals. You have to find out where they put them and get them back. Please, it's my only chance. I don't have anyone else."

"Stay still." She paused and then realized what she just said; she tried to cover an embarrassed smile with her hand. "I'm sorry. Look, I'll see what I can find. Hang in there."

With that she quickly left the room. Garruty felt his heart sag; he was now left with what seemed like a capricious hope. He closed his eyes and tried to relax.

Later that afternoon, a nurse disturbed his nervous rest. She was African-American, young and athletically built. In an unusually cheery voice she said, "Well, Mr. Garruty, the doctors have decided it's time for you to try some solid food. We have to get you back to feeling better, you know?"

She adjusted the motorized bed until he was in an upright sitting position and set the tray in his lap. He looked down at the three small dishes and the glass of juice. Despite his hunger pangs, he could see the poison molecules floating in every food item on the tray.

"I don't think I can keep anything down. I feel queasy, and, and really dizzy."

The nurse quickly removed the tray. "Do you want to lie back again?" she asked.

"Ooohhh, please," he groaned as best he could.

The nurse checked his IV; he closed his eyes and faked nodding off. He could tell she stayed a while, no doubt observing him, but she finally left. He tried once more to free himself of the cursed straps, but to no avail. Before long he fell asleep again.

While Garruty was asleep, the two guards on watch were fixing coffee in a small snack room not far from his room. The heavy-set older one stirred his steaming cup, pushed his glasses up and spoke. "You know, I think Mr. Garruty's deranged. I heard one of the FBI agents say he'd read some of the poor fellow's journals, and Garruty actually wrote in there that he was..." he paused to blow his hot coffee, "...sure the FBI was going to terminate him!"

At that moment, Carmela Ortiz was about to pass by the snack room and overheard Garruty's name spoken. She stopped at the edge of the doorway and held her ear closer. All she heard was, "...sure the FBI was going to terminate him!" She quickly turned and headed for Garruty's room.

After four fitful hours of sleep, Garruty awoke to see Carmela tiptoe up to the side of his bed. He could tell she was nervous. "What's up? Did you find my books?" he asked impatiently.

"Hush and listen. I'm going to get you out of here. Just be really quiet. I overheard the guards talking. They were saying something about the FBI terminating you! They're away on break right now, and the hallways are empty. If you want your notebooks, they're in room 212B, next floor down. We can get them, but we better be quick about it."

While Carmela pulled out his IV, Garruty started thinking. If I was the carrier, wouldn't Carmela be showing symptoms by now? She seems fine. Maybe... maybe I'm not the one.

Carmela undid the straps and helped Garruty sit up. He was unstable and almost toppled forward on his first attempt to take a step. Slowly he regained his balance and they exited the room. She grabbed his backpack from the temporary interrogation room on second floor and they snuck out the back of the hospital. Within a half hour they were at her apartment.

Over the next three days, under Carmela's expert care, Garruty began to get some of his strength back. They decided he needed some exercise, so on the fourth day she took him for a walk on some of the secluded streets in the neighborhood. Along a narrow street lined with bushes, near a private school, they saw three young boys with sticks, poking at something in a bush.

When they got close, Carmela said, "It looks like they're after some kind of insect."

Garruty walked up behind the trio of blue-jeaned, tennis-shoed investigators just as one of them was rearing back with his stick, undoubtedly getting ready to deliver a major blow to the already disturbed insect. By this time, Garruty could see that it was a nearly full-grown praying mantis.

"You think that bug can sting?" he asked.

The boy turned toward Garruty and lowered the stick. "It looks yucky, mister," he replied.

"Well, looks aren't everything. Just look at Herman Munster. He was pretty scary looking. But didn't you like him? He was my favorite because his facial expressions showed that he was kind and caring."

Carmela piped up, "Let's take a close look at it. Maybe it's a good bug."

The boys joined Garruty and Carmela as they slowly approached the praying mantis. At age six, and living in the city, they didn't have much experience with bugs.

The one blond boy said, "Don't be scared ya'll."

Now confronted by five ridiculously huge forms, the brave mantis reared up on its middle and hind legs and poised its enlarged, raptorial front legs; it cocked its head toward them in almost human-like fashion.

Garruty whispered, "Oh, it's a praying mantis! Yes, a very good bug! It eats flies and mosquitoes and other pesky little bugs. We should always make sure praying mantises are protected, don't you think?"

"Yeah," chimed in the boys, wide eyed.

Garruty tried to reinforce his argument. "We're very lucky to see a praying mantis. Maybe one of you can make a drawing of it and the three of you can tell the other students in your class about it."

As the boys looked at each other, Garruty could tell wheels of thought were turning inside their heads. They put down their sticks and headed for the school, chattering as they went. Carmela turned to Garruty, a pleased look on her face.

He looked at her and said, "I wish someday people in this country would realize what fantastic insects these are and revere them like the Japanese do."

Carmela took his hand and said, "Come, there's something you should see."

They walked without speaking for a few blocks, turned left, and then proceeded down a narrow alley for another block. She led him up a narrow stone stairway on the backside of an old stone building. At the top of the stairs, the stones surrounded a small marble patio. Carmela turned Garruty around so that he was looking at the building across the alleyway. He was so astonished that his mouth opened but he was at a loss for words. Right there in front of him was a 12-foot long metal sculpture of a praying mantis, in a superb life-like pose. The detail was incredible, right down to the spines on the legs and the network of veins on the wings. The copper metal had turned partly green, adding to the effect.

"Come on, let's go down so you can take a closer look. This is the pantheon where I have been going every other Saturday for the past six months. The main idea," she explained, "is to gain greater respect for each other by first learning to respect other living things. The praying mantis symbolizes reverence for all living things."

"That seems so natural," he said. "I could get into that."

On the way back to her apartment, Carmela asked Garruty how he got the nickname "Pancake." Before he could answer, she said, "It can't be because you ate a record number of pancakes, can it?"

"No, I've never overeaten anything. No, that name goes back to my graduate school days. See, when I got interested in dragonflies, I had to collect some of them for detailed study. I had trouble catching them with my net while they were flying, so I invented the method of flopping my net over them while they were perched flat on the ground. A fellow student termed this "pan caking" and somehow the nickname Pancake got started. You know how graduate students are, it stuck."

After dinner that night, Carmela asked Garruty about his career. He glossed over most of his accomplishments and then told her about his recent struggles, starting with contracting poison ivy in New Jersey. He finally explained why he was flown to Atlanta and revealed to her his fear of being a carrier of the disease. He stressed how he hated the suspicion that surrounded him.

"Maybe you're not a carrier," Carmela interrupted. "People who've contracted the virus show symptoms in 24 to 48 hours. Look, I've been near you for over four days and I am not sick!"

Garruty breathed a sigh of relief. She was right. But, he thought, the FBI doesn't know that.

The next morning Garruty told Carmela about some of the strange turns his life had taken since he retired, even disclosing some of his recent experiences with insects. He told her that he was still pretty confused about some of the things that had happened. When she asked how he could have traveled back in time, he told her he wasn't sure and then launched into revealing his most recent puzzling encounters. He dwelled particularly on the Great Lakes fireflies and how they led him to the legendary figure, Hutsonwatha, at the bottom of Lake Huron.

"It was later the next morning when I heard about the manhunt on the radio and that they were looking for me."

Upon hearing about this escapade, Carmela, with a puzzled look, questioned whether he heard the entire radio broadcast that morning he woke up on the shore near Cedarville.

She held her hands out with palms up and said, "Well, however you got to that sandy shore... Look, I don't know, but I think the CDC was looking for you at that time to find out why you were immune. Don't you think they'd want to get a blood sample from you and analyze the antibodies your body had produced? That would help them develop a cure, which would hopefully put up a barrier to further infections. The spinal tap would help them determine the virus's genetic makeup. I think the media was pleading for you to report to a hospital."

Garruty wasn't convinced. He thought, She means well, but she's fallen for their ploy.

During their time together, Garruty thought how easy it would be to fall in love with Carmela, and how much he would like that. Jenine had rekindled something inside him, a realization that he could again find love in his life. He wondered if Carmela could fall in love with him. That thought set off a warning bell—he was quite a bit older than she, and he might still be in trouble. I can't get that close, not right now.

One morning Carmela said, "It's Saturday. There's a meeting this morning at the pantheon, at ten o'clock. Want to go with me?"

"Sure," he replied.

As they sat and listened to the leaders of the discussion, Garruty became more and more disinterested. Instead of exploring ways in which people could get along better, they were centering on the evils of man. It was getting close to being confrontational. Garruty whispered to Carmela a plea to leave early and she agreed.

When they got outside, she confided, "I don't know. They've been like this lately, getting more abrasive. I might not come back."

When they got to the corner just before her apartment, Carmela told Garruty she needed a few things from the pharmacy. While Garruty waited outside, several police officers and plainclothesmen knocked on her apartment door. One of them had only one arm. Sure could be Agent Booker. I bet that missing arm is the one where the wasps stung him. Garruty slipped around the corner. He went into the drug store and faked looking for something in order to stall Carmela who was about ready to leave. Before they were through in the store, he suggested they go out for lunch, thinking the gendarmes would surely be gone by the time they got back.

Luckily Carmela said, "That sounds like fun."

That evening, they stepped out on the terrace of her apartment and sat in a small swing. The sun was sinking below the horizon, a signal to Garruty that time was running out. Carmela put her arms around his right arm and rested her head on his shoulder. "So what's your favorite bug?" she asked.

He knew she used the term bug in an affectionate way, so he didn't mind. Most people used the term in a derogatory way, and that was a big pet peeve of his.

"Well, I have a lot of favorites, but I have to say that the Luna Flies are Number 1."

"Luna Flies? Oh, do you mean Luna Moths?"

"No, Luna Flies."

"I've never heard of them. What do they look like?"

"Oh, there's nothing else like them. They have long, narrow transparent wings supported by wavy white veins, and there are long orange streamers on the hind pair. They can fold their wings and tuck them inside their long, streamlined, torpedo-shaped bodies. And they have shields over their eyes. See, all that's necessary for the long journey to earth and back."

"To earth?"

"Why yes," Garruty whispered, lowering his voice. "They make the trip every synodical month. Yep, one round trip every 29 days, 12 hours, and 44 minutes. The journey to earth takes exactly one week. They arrive in the evening, just when the moon is at its maximum fullness when viewed from earth. First they sip nectar from Wild Passion Flowers to rejuvenate themselves, and then they mate. Before morning, they start on the trip back to the moon. That's why most people don't know about them; you see, they have to get back right away to lay their eggs and raise their young, the next generation."

"But what's up there on the moon for bugs to eat?" she asked.

"Cheese," Garruty answered.

She smiled and looked toward the horizon, seeing the huge, glowing, orange colored sphere with new eyes. "They must almost be here now," she said softly.

"Any time now. Do you have any Passion Flowers nearby?"

She turned toward him and whispered, "There must be lots of them around, the way I feel tonight."

Their eyes met. There was a moment of silence and then Garruty said, "Carmela, I'm indebted to you for saving my life, and for being there for me. I've never met anyone as precious as you are. I feel..." but he stopped and paused. "I hate to have to tell you this—I have to leave the country for a while. As soon as possible."

"Why? What is it with you?" She put her head down and put her hands over her forehead. She looked up again and added in exasperation, "You can stay here; no one will find you! Besides, if you're immune, you could be the answer to finding a cure."

But Garruty still believed that somehow the FBI and CIA still intended to eliminate him. "I'm not taking any chances. They've been able to track me down wherever I've gone here in the states. Why take a chance? If I leave, maybe they'll think I died and they'll ease up. Look, I'll come back; everything will be all right."

Carmela sighed and finally gave in. There was a chance he was right, plus she just didn't have the energy or right words to argue with this man anymore.

"If I can get to Ecuador, I've got a friend there who can find a place for me to stay. It'll be like I disappeared. But I don't know how I'll get to Miami. It'll be too risky to get a commercial flight at Hartsfield International Airport."

She now knew that using logic to reason with him in this paranoid state was futile, and she decided it would be best to assist him with a plan. Fortunately Carmela knew that Savoy Nickols, with whom she had become acquainted at the temple, had a private plane. The next day she called him and found out that he was scheduled to fly down to Florida the following week. She asked if he could take a friend of hers to Miami. She sensed the hesitation in his voice, but when she told him that Garruty would more than compensate him, he agreed.

The drive to meet Savoy was mostly silent. Garruty finally spoke. "I know you're fed up with me. You probably won't want to see me again, ever."

Carmela stopped the car at the last traffic light before the turn onto the road leading to Savoy's hangar. She turned to look at him, this time directly into his searching blue eyes. He looked so eager for an answer. He was a kitten in an animal shelter, waiting for that special person with warm eyes to come by and say, "I'm taking that one home."

She realized this could be the last time she ever saw him. She brushed away her tears and replied, "I just...I'm afraid I'll never see you again." New tears trickled down her smooth cheeks. "I vowed I'd never again make anyone promise me anything, but..." (she stopped to sniff), "are you coming back?"

Garruty's heart melted; he hadn't thought that at this point in his life someone could really care about him. He put his hand on hers and fought back his own tears. "I'll only be gone a month or two. I'll be back."

No more was said as Carmela pulled her car toward the hangar and stopped.

8

Escape to Chinchipino

The instant the right rear window in Carmela's car shattered, Garruty bailed out. There was no time for a tenderhearted good-bye. As he slammed the car door shut, he yelled to her, "Get going!"

It was a good thing they were late getting to the airstrip, as Savoy already had his Cessna Caravan ready for takeoff. When Garruty saw the small commuter plane on the runway with the prop turning, he changed course and headed for it in a zigzag path.

"Savoy?"

"Yeah. Garruty?"

"Yeah. Hit it," Garruty shouted as he jumped in and slammed the door shut. He tossed his backpack behind the seat and fastened his seatbelt. He looked back and saw Carmela's car streak around the hangar and speed down a back road.

"What happened back there?" Savoy asked as he pushed the throttle and guided the plane into the air.

Garruty didn't want Savoy to know the FBI was after him, fearing he'd undoubtedly change his mind about taking him to Miami. "Oh, road rage, pure and simple. We must have ticked that guy off when he cut in front of us at that last turn. I mouthed off to him, well, through the windshield. Man, talk about a short fuse. He followed us and threw a rock at me and hit Carmela's back window. She'll be all right, it looks like he's not following her."

"Man, people nowadays," said Savoy. "You got to be careful man."

Savoy was middle-aged, and apparently quite well to do. His classy white slacks and gray silk shirt were evidence that he liked the finer things in life. Judging from the man's features, Garruty knew he was Hispanic before he heard his accent.

Except for some tummy-tingling turbulence over north Florida, the three-hour flight to Miami went pretty smooth. They had trouble finding things to talk about at first. Savoy continued talking about people's attitudes.

"What bugs me the most is the disrespect. It doesn't matter if they know you or not, people don't care about anyone anymore."

Garruty was offended by his use of the word "bugs". He couldn't stand that transfer of meaning, that demeaning usage for whatever bothered people. Sure, he thought, some bugs do bother us, but most are harmless and many are beneficial. Geez, from cold 'bugs' to computer 'bugs', insects get a bad rap. He decided not to lecture Savoy.

There was another stiff lull in the conversation, but then Savoy mentioned he was glad that the Santana epidemic had not gotten to Atlanta yet. Garruty had not kept up with the spread of the disease for a couple of weeks. The exchange picked up rapidly.

"Santana? How did it get that name?" he asked.

Savoy answered, "Man, haven't you been keeping up with the news? They named it 'Santana virus' after the town in Alabama where it first showed up."

Garruty thought about home. "How far has it gotten?"

"Up north, it's spread east all the way to New York, and it's as far west as Montana. But down south here, where it apparently started, it spread faster to the west than eastward. Apparently it hasn't gotten to south Florida yet either," said Savoy.

During the rest of the flight they talked about other diseases, politics, war, and the stock market, although neither brought up the topic of the weather. The whole time Garruty was thinking mostly about the Miami Airport. The FBI could easily have agents waiting there to spot him and take him into custody. Even if I slip past them, how am I going to get a ticket to Ecuador? Maybe if I pay Savoy extra, he'll go in and purchase a ticket for me. No, he'd have to show my passport. I'll just have to take a chance and go up to the ticket counter. Maybe if I wore a different hat, or better yet, changed my look somehow until I get up to the line.

As they flew over Miami and made the approach to the small commuter runway, the rear of the plane was buffeted by a gusty cross wind. When it looked like they were going to come down sideways, Garruty put a death grip on his seat cushion. But Savoy's skills as a pilot were up to the challenge and he set the wheels down on the runway like pushing a baby carriage on a carpeted walkway. They rolled to a stop and looked at each other.

"Thanks Savoy, for the ride and the conversation," he said. Garruty paid him in cash, giving him an extra hundred dollars.

"No problem, nice meeting you. Hey, I'm heading back to Atlanta day after tomorrow if you need a ride back."

"No thanks, I'm going to be here for a while. Take care," Garruty replied as he picked up his backpack and left.

The first order of business was to take a taxi into Miami and find a shopping mall. He bought a pair of sunglasses, some supplies and a few extra light clothes suitable for the tropical climate. Garruty then set to work on his planned "look". First he got a haircut, and then he found a store that sold facial disguise items. Twenty minutes in the dressing room and he was ready. Entering Miami International Airport, he looked older, bent over, bald, with a slender gray mustache and gray eyebrows.

Once inside level 1 of the huge U-shaped terminal building, he tried to stay among crowds of people to be as inconspicuous as possible. Near the main terminal, he entered a men's room and took off his disguise. He sauntered up to the line leading to the American Airlines ticket counter and sat on his backpack to keep a low profile while he waited. He noticed a lady near the front of the line reading a newspaper and saw his picture on the front page. The caption read, "This Man Wanted By The FBI." He was a nervous wreck by the time he reached the counter. However, he got the last seat available on the next flight to Quito, departing at 8:00 a.m. the next morning. At the security gate, the guards singled him out and even searched his shoes. He couldn't believe they let him through.

After that he found a place to sit and breathed a big sigh of relief. Slipped through so far; you must be living right, he thought, but he knew he wouldn't relax until his flight was airborne. He called Carmela and to make sure she was all right and to tell her he would be leaving in the morning for Ecuador. After they said good-bye, he hoped he would someday hear her voice again right next to him.

Except for midday turbulence from gigantic, billowing black thermals over Colombia, the four-hour flight to Ecuador went smoothly. Garruty caught up in his journal and dozed off at intervals. When he woke up for the fifth time, he looked out his window and saw Quito, the capital city, nestled in a narrow valley at 10,000 feet altitude. Through the huge, broken clouds, he saw the distant snow-covered peaks of Cayambe to the east and Cotopaxi to the south. The plane landed in light rain and slowly taxied to the International Terminal of Quito's Aeropuerto Mariscal Sucre.

Garruty had no problems going through immigration and customs.

"Avenida Santa Rosa, 315 ½, por favor. Es cerca Ritter y La Universidad," Garruty informed the diminutive taxi driver, as he breathed deeply in the high thin air. He had been to Quito several times, and he wanted the driver to know he still remembered the city so as to avoid a long drive and an inflated taxi fare.

"Si, señor."

The high metal wall surrounding Angel Olivarius's premises was secured by a double heavy metal gate reinforced with iron bars and a built-in lock. Garruty pushed a button that he assumed rang a bell inside. After a couple of minutes Dr. Olivarius appeared.

"It is good to see you again, Dr. Garruty. I am glad you call from airport, so I can be here," said Angel. "Mi ingles still not so good yet."

"Hola Angel. ¿Como estas, mi amigo? My Spanish is not as good as your English!"

"Ha-ha. Come in. You must to stay with us tonight. Then tomorrow we make the plans for you travel. ¿Tiene hambre?"

"Si, but I hope it's not a bother."

"No, no, we are making dinner now. You must to meet my wife. Come, I help you with your, your, (pause) how you say equipaje?"

"Ah, luggage. Gracias, I don't have much."

The spaghetti dinner and fresh bread was the best meal Garruty had eaten in a year. The lemon grass tea afterwards was "for the digestion," as Angel said. Angel's wife, Ferina, was short and light of stature, being mixed Quichua and Spanish. She did not speak any English and quietly went about cleaning up while Angel and Garruty talked about their insect studies.

That evening, when he finally retired to bed, Garruty felt chilly, even though Ferina made sure he had a wool blanket. But the heavy covers and thin air made for poor sleeping. He had another problem. His recurring dreams alternated between traveling back in time to an ancient steamy jungle in which predators appeared everywhere he went and his being stranded high on the glaciers of Mt. Cotopaxi. The morning light was a welcome sight.

That morning, Angel made the arrangements for Garruty's trip to the jungle in the western part of the upper Amazon basin, the Oriente. One of his older students, Ernesto, was told to accompany Garruty to make sure he got there safely and to make the final preparations at the place where he would be staying. That afternoon the two new acquaintances took a bus from Quito to the mountain town of Baeza. The ride through the surrounding forested mountains and valleys of the Andes Mountains filled Garruty with wonder; the waterfalls, some of which fell several hundred feet, were spectacular.

That night they stayed in a small hotel, the Residencial Nadial. They had dinner together, and in mixed English and Spanish talked about the tropical rain forest and its diverse fauna. He found out that Ernesto was researching the different native peoples of the Oriente to find out what knowledge of insects they had before the Spanish conquistadors arrived, even before the Inca had taken them over. The next morning the two new friends took a small bus south to Tena. There they hired a taxi to take them to Puerto Napo and then east to Misahuallí. At the jungle lodge, Ernesto arranged a trip down the Rio Napo in a dugout canoe to get them to their final destination, the forest village called Chinchipino.

Garruty was in awe of the breadth of the Rio Napo. It was hard to believe that the Napo was merely a tributary of the mighty Amazon. Across the great expanse of churning muddy water the grand ceiba trees on the opposite bank looked like miniature facsimiles on a model railroad scene, and their loosely draped lianas seemed like slender, looping threads. The anticipation of smelling, seeing, touching and hearing the rain forest up close again heightened his awareness. He was fed up with traveling and ready for biological adventure, however small. He was glad it wasn't raining. The small outboard motor chugged and belched bluish gray smoke, at times cutting out and having to be restarted. Garruty preferred the slow river-driven drifting of the crude canoe to that of the loud, polluting man-made source of power. He glanced at the worn, uneven edges of the hand-made canoe and imagined the severe slivers it must have delivered when it was newly hewn. Such thoughts were interrupted every once in a while by a glimpse of a large dark dragonfly skimming close over the water's surface.

When one of the dragonflies hovered particularly close to the boat, he inquired under his breath, "What are you doing way out here?" He imagined it saying, "Looking for you." Then he noticed Ernesto leaning toward him from behind, mouthing, "I see them too." Garruty wondered what they didn't see.

They had to cross the daunting river in order to get to Chinchipino, and Garruty was impressed with the skill with which the river men guided the boat, angling toward the far bank. As they pulled close, he saw the small river after which the village was named. The Rio Chinchipino was a narrow, sparkling jewel that meandered through heavy rain forest. The small village was situated a short distance from its mouth so that none of the dwellings were visible from the big river. The dwellings were widely scattered; there were no streets, only small trails between huts, as there were no vehicles. He wondered what the people did for a living, as he saw no large cut-and-burn openings in the forest.

Ernesto spoke to the boatmen and told Garruty how much he owed them in Sucres. He then met with the chief of the village, Quallillo, and began to work out the details for Garruty's stay.

"How long you be here?" he asked Garruty.

"Maybe two months, I have a lot of work to do."

Ernesto spoke to the chief in a language Garruty did not recognize. He realized communication was going to be a real problem. Maybe I can learn some of their words and teach them some English, he thought. After what seemed like at least an hour of discussion between the two men, Ernesto came over to where Garruty was sitting.

"You to stay en una cabaña, the name es Tahuansuyo."

"Ta-huan-suyo," Garruty repeated slowly.

"Si, it is that way, en la selva," Ernesto said pointing toward the lush growth. "Es cerca del arroyo; very nice for you! You be near Torres family. You must help them with some chores, but you have much time to do your studies."

"Claro." Garruty picked up his belongings and followed Ernesto for a few hundred yards along the trail to the cabaña.

Because it was nearly 6:00 p.m., the time of sunset every day near the equator, Ernesto stayed with Garruty that evening. They shared a light meal of mainly vegetables and fruit with the Torres family. The father Kali and mother Telina welcomed them, although their two young boys, Tejillo and Kalsuyo, peered at Garruty with large, dark, almost sad eyes, in utter silence. The conversation was totally alien to Garruty. He felt left out, except that by watching their gestures, he guessed that insects were somehow included in the discussion. At one point, Kali held his hands more than a foot apart, indicating to Ernesto how big something was. He then put his arms out with elbows bent and moved them as if mimicking something walking in a herky-jerky manner. Although Ernesto nodded as if he understood, the look on his face was one of disbelief.

Early the next morning, Ernesto was ready to return to the University in Quito. "Muchas gracias, Ernesto. You are coming back in two months?" Garruty asked.

"Si, I come again to help, two months."

The dugout canoe sputtered in a tug-of-war with the clay-laden water but slowly crept upstream. Ernesto turned and waved. Garruty didn't want him to leave; a lonely, almost desperate feeling washed over him. Like an animal in new surroundings, he felt a need for familiarity, a need to establish a home base. He decided to go back to the cabaña and get organized. As he made his way past the small, flimsy huts, he felt countless eyes crawl over his skin. He walked purposefully and for the most part looked down at the path. With each step, the yearning for acceptance grew stronger, but he felt as if they were suspicious of him.

After he arranged his things in the cabaña, he walked over to the small stream. He squatted, cautious not to sit on something that housed a million defense-minded ants. He was glad it wasn't raining. After a few minutes trying to collect his thoughts, he felt as if he were being watched. He slowly turned his head and saw Tejillo and Kalsuyo peering at him from behind a tree. How can I get those little ones to trust me? How do I communicate with them?

Garruty made a quarter turn and knelt, sitting on his heels. He picked up a small dead twig and started to draw in the sand. First he drew a rough image of a flower with five petals. Next he drew an image of a bee hovering above the flower. He looked over at the boys and smiled. Tejillo, the slightly larger one, and who Garruty guessed was probably eight, stepped from behind the tree. He grabbed his younger brother's hand and they approached slowly, stopping about six feet away. Garruty pointed the stick at one of the petals in his drawing and held up one finger. He then pointed to the next petal and held up two fingers. He kept going until he got to number five. The boys looked puzzled. Garruty held up one finger and touched one petal as he said "Uno."

No reaction. Garruty paused and scratched his head. He then drew the numeral "1" in the sand. Kalsuyo came forward and with his finger drew the numeral "2" next to it. Garruty smiled at the boy and was about to draw the numeral "3" when Tejillo took the stick from Garruty and pointed to the drawing of the bee.

"Sizi," he said and began to draw in the sand. The image was unmistakable — it was a stick insect. Garruty was impressed at how large Tejillo had portrayed the insect, nearly as long as his arm. Garruty pointed at the drawing and looked questionably at Tejillo. "Puitlo," replied the boy, pointing up at the trees.

Kalsuyo repeated, "Ooh, Puitlo."

Even though Garruty didn't put much stock in what the boys were indicating, he was glad to be making progress toward meaningful interchange. He was especially impressed with Tejillo's artistic ability. He slowly reached into his backpack and pulled out two Boston Red Sox baseball caps and placed them on the boys' heads. He helped them adjust the size, and then looked at them and nodded. "Lookin' good," he said.

The boys finally smiled. Garruty stood up, moaning as his aging knees cracked. They each put a hand in his and the trio walked toward the Torres family hut. Must be time for breakfast, Garruty thought.

Over the next few days, Garruty and the two jungle boys spent a lot of time together. Instead of trying to teach them English, he told them his name was Amos and he tried to learn their words for basic things. They showed him the chores they had to do, such as composting organic waste produced by the villagers and conditioning seeds of various trees for later planting. Garruty discovered that there was very little he could show them. He found they had knowledge of and respect for other living things that he had never seen in children before. Moreover, Tejillo's potential in visual arts and little Kalsuyo's aptitude in mathematics became evident. If I had had children of my own, I wonder what kind of father I would have been? How could that have been possible with a woman who only thought of fashion and herself? Would it have been like this, experiencing those precious moments when they wondered and discovered? All he knew was that he saw something special in these two boys, something he never knew he was missing.

One day Garruty showed the boys how dragonflies mate and where they lay their eggs. "Amoses" Tejillo called them. I guess if they don't have a name for something, they make one up, thought Garruty. When they found one emerging on a damp log, he wanted them to see it close up. He looked in his backpack for his hand lens, but it wasn't there. Then he remembered the last time he used it.

"Oh man, I must've left it in the crack of the big rock at Clifton. I have to get it back," he murmured, thinking about its sentimental value. His major professor, Dr. Herod Quirk, gave it to him when he earned his Ph.D. degree, but then the professor mysteriously disappeared. Garruty was glad he packed a 3X magnifying glass, enough to allow the boys to see the insect better. Gosh, 'ooh wee' must be the universal expression for glee, he thought.

By the second week of his stay, Garruty had discovered over 20 species of dragonflies along the Rio Chinchipino, plus he found where they laid their eggs and their exact larval habitat. He filled page after page in his field notebook with detailed observations and was feeling quite content, especially because the data fit nicely into his new theory on the dynamics of insect distributions.

However, there was a problem of another kind that Garruty was experiencing. After a few days of eating the local food, his digestive system had gone on the fritz and he had to make a tough decision. He had packed enough anti-diarrhea medicine for only a couple days. He could take it and have the problem reappear, or he could tough it out right then and hope to become immune. He had decided on the latter, but after a week of the trots, he was getting dehydrated. In desperation, he tried to explain his problem to Kali and Telina; embarrassed, he had to pantomime to get them to understand. After a few chuckles, they gave him a homemade concoction of different plant extracts, and within half a day, Garruty was cured.

Garruty was so thankful that he made an effort to learn more about these people. In particular, he noticed that the slash and burn clearings he had seen all over the tropics were nonexistent here. Instead, these people grew vegetables in small plots in the forest and set out isolated fruit trees in strategic places so as not to diminish the forest. It appeared that after growing vegetables in an area for a few months, they prepared the disturbed plot for reforestation. This was just part of their harmonious relationship with all the living things of the forest.

But there was another feature of this society that was difficult for Garruty to believe. After Garruty had gained a fair understanding of their language, Chief Quallillo and Kali explained that they did not let their village's population level exceed the environment's carrying capacity for human beings. They were aware that the human species could escape natural population checks, allowing human populations to increase and outstrip the local environment's carrying capacity. On top of this, too many people led to concentration of wastes, which could cause severe environmental problems. When this happened, many other species could no longer coexist. Therefore, the village's birth and immigration rates were controlled.

What stunned Garruty the most was the implication of how they learned all this. Quallillo summoned Tejillo, gave him parchment and charcoal, and ordered him to draw. Within 20 minutes, Tejillo presented Garruty with a magnificent illustration of a giant walking stick. *That's like the drawing he made in the sand that first day, and it's the same size. It's huge, maybe a foot and a half long!* he thought. Garruty tried to indicate that the insect must be smaller, maybe half that size at most. All present shook their heads and pointed to the drawing. "Actual size" Garruty translated their response.

Quallillo explained. "The stick insect taught our ancestors how to live in peace and harmony within the forest. As generations passed, they saw that the guidance of the giant walking sticks worked and we now have great adulation for them and all insects. We also communicate with other forest creatures, but the giant walking sticks continuously provide the measure and adjustment of our village population."

The actuality of a people living in harmony in this rain forest occupied Garruty's thoughts for the next several days. Who really taught these people such strict ecological principles? And not only the principles, but how to actually make them work? Could some missionary who was also a population ecologist have visited them? But why do they insist that the stick insects were responsible? He thought about the cult in Atlanta revering the praying mantis. Then Garruty suddenly realized something. If there really is some kind of large stick insect around here, I can see why Quallillo has been especially suspicious of me. Just to be safe, if I see a big walking stick, I'll leave it alone. But they've got me curious now.

Garruty continued to spend time with the two boys, but he also continued studying the insect fauna of the Rio Chinchipino. With about a week left before he was to return to Quito, he decided to venture alone as far upstream as he could go. It was a sunny morning, the first in several weeks, and he felt good.

"The all-natural, unprocessed food I've been eating, with its lack of preservatives, must have cleansed my system," he mused.

He had also gotten quite a bit of rest the last month. The adventure of seeing unexplored jungle with his every step had his adrenaline flowing. Upstream the trees were alive with many different kinds of birds, and colorful butterflies and dragonflies flitted away and perched high in bushes and trees along the edges when he disturbed their hiding places. Within an hour he saw nine different families of damselflies, twice as many as occurred in all of North America. Several so-called helicopters, representing the largest damselflies in existence, floated down intermittent sunbeams penetrating the tree canopy. One in particular had large bright yellow spots on its wing tips that gave the impression of two pairs of sulfur butterflies flying in unison.

Maybe I'm in heaven, he thought. I must be, I haven't even seen a mosquito, much less gotten bitten. He had been worried that if mosquitoes took his blood, they might become infected with the virus and put the people of the village at risk.

After a couple of hours of exploring, the stream began to narrow noticeably. At one point, he came to a dead tree trunk about 16 inches in diameter, draped across the entire stream width. Garruty noticed that it was covered with epiphytes; he didn't inspect it closely, he just wanted to get around it. It was too high to step over, so he bent down and agonizingly scrunched underneath it. When he straightened up, he realized he was covered with dozens of army ants. They must have been marching across the fallen tree, using it for a bridge, he thought. The sight of the sickle-jawed soldiers reminded him of the Memorial Day trial and the dreadful queen. Quickly brushing them off, he reminded himself, Don't panic, you've stood right in their trails before and had them all over your trousers. But he vowed to be more watchful and not take his mind completely off his surroundings.

Garruty noticed that the character of the stream had changed. There was more underbrush along the edge, and the tree canopy was less dense, making it brighter at ground level. At a slower, deeper stretch of the stream, he slowly waded along the edge. He bent down to see if there were any damselflies hiding within the tangles of vines. When he straightened back up, he felt something clinging to his bare arm; it gave the impression of something large. Startled at first, he saw that it was a walking stick, and a giant one at that! Its front feet clung to the back of his left hand and the tip of its abdomen was up by his shoulder. It slowly raised its long antennae and turned around to face Garruty. The sheer size of an insect that big perched on his arm gave Garruty the willies, but then he realized that walking sticks were harmless. He moved his right index finger toward its head, and the insect swayed back.

"Whoa, big guy," Garruty heard a low soft voice say. He looked around and saw no one. The wood-colored stick tapped the padded feet at the ends of its long front legs on Garruty's hand. "You taste weird." There was a pause. "You are a stranger here; what you should realize is that everything the people of Chinchipino told you is true. We work together so all beings who make their home here can survive. My species lives here, but oversees all in Chinchipino."

Garruty was dumbstruck. He stared at the huge insect, thinking, I must have new eyes, new ears. He asked, "I'm supposed to believe that there's no human intelligence involved in this, just you? You control the populations?"

"Tell me anywhere on earth that humans have not outstripped their environment. Humans are an oxymoron—the most intelligent, most ignorant species rolled into one."

Garruty conceded. He thought, All our knowledge, all our technology, and all the warnings; what good has it done? With each advance, we take a step backward.

He involuntarily lowered his arm and brushed up against the tangled vines. "Enough?" the walking stick asked, and Garruty nodded. The huge insect purposefully crawled onto several long stems and within seconds was undetectable. Garruty stared at the vegetation for awhile longer, then turned and started back toward the village, preoccupied with thoughts of the unique insect-man relationship. A light rain started to fall, but within half an hour, it turned to a steady downpour. By the time he returned to the cabaña, he was so drenched his fingertips were white and wrinkled.

He went inside and grabbed a towel, thinking, Has the secret to the long-term survival of the human species just been revealed to me? During the next few days, he talked with the villagers, trying to pry out more details, wondering if their way of life could work in a more developed society.

It appeared that the people didn't have anything to add to what he had already learned, but merely went about their daily tasks, not planning ahead, not worrying about the future. He began to doubt if they were in control of their own birth rate, and whether they had the liberty to think for themselves.

A few days later, early in the morning, as he sat at the mouth of the river, the unmistakable sputtering of a certain outboard motor interrupted Garruty's thoughts. He looked up and saw Ernesto waving from the dugout canoe.

"Ah, mi amigo," he shouted. It felt good to see Ernesto again, as if a connection with the real world had been restored.

"Are you finish your studies," Ernesto asked.

"Si, I need a hamburger."

Ernesto laughed, but he understood. As they loaded Garruty's belongings into the boat, the people slowly sauntered to the river's edge to see him off. After dozens of short good-byes, the dugout turned and headed upstream. Garruty leaned over to Ernesto and said, "You should maybe visit the people of Chinchipino again to learn more about their knowledge of insects and their relationship with them." Ernesto nodded. Two days later they were in Quito.

"You must to visit more often," Angel insisted.

"I'd like that. Take care, my friend, and thank you for everything," replied Garruty.

The flight to Mexico City was so rough that Garruty had second thoughts about his plan for getting back into the United States. I hope Ramiro is still at the university, and that he'll be able to help me get to the border. He also contemplated the society in the little village perched at the edge of the Rio Napo. Suddenly he realized, Such a system could never get started in an already crowded society. Besides, the giant walking sticks are endemic to Chinchipino; they would be unable to exist anywhere else. I'm not telling anybody about this—heck, no one would believe me anyway!

9

Butterfly High

Ramiro Morales couldn't believe his eyes. "It must be 10 years since I see you, Pancake," he howled. "What brings you here?"

The two old friends shook hands vigorously as their eyes locked in mutual respect. When they were much younger, they spent several years together in northern Mexico, searching for natural enemies of insect pests of cotton. An encounter they had while traversing remote lands in the state of Durango had welded these two men into an everlasting blood-brother relationship.

"I need your help, Ramiro. Can you get me to the border?"

"Ah, more bandidos after you, amigo?"

"More like federales, hermano. Listen, I'd like to get all the way to Sonora, but even if you could help me get as far as Sinaloa, that would be great. I really hate to ask," replied Garruty.

On the way to Mexico, Garruty had thought about his connection with Ramiro. Vivid memories of that frightful incident in Durango flashed through his mind. Captured by a gang of outlaws, they were being held without food or water in an isolated adobe hut. Ramiro and Garruty had nothing of value on their persons, and the bandidos were obviously angry and frustrated. On the afternoon of the third day of captivity, two of the men entered the small hut and yanked Ramiro up off the floor. They hoisted him up by the ropes that bound his wrists. As he hung there like an animal, they pulled off his shirt. The largest of the men then pulled a machete and readied to swing full force at Ramiro's midsection. In a split second, Garruty sprang to his feet and lurched forward, and with his hands tied in front of him, he drove his shoulder into the man's stomach. As they tumbled to the dirt floor, Garruty grabbed the machete and waved it wildly about the small room, spitting and cursing. The bandidos scurried out of the hut. Garruty quickly cut Ramiro down and they ran out the back. His memory of the rest of their harrowing escape had blurred, even though he had nightmares about that hut for years afterwards.

Ramiro hesitated for a moment and then replied, "Sure, anything for you, my friend. I'll need some time to get ready, maybe only a day or two. And I have to tell my wife. OK?"

"Yes, no great hurry. I really..."

"You don't have to say anything. Hey, let's go way around Durango, what do you say?" Ramiro suggested as he moved his left hand in a large semicircle.

"Good thinking," said Garruty.

Ramiro reserved his favorite vehicle, an old Range Rover, from the Geology Department at the University. The next day, they were ready to roll.

As they wound their way out of the narrow, confusing streets of Mexico City, Garruty was glad Ramiro was driving.

"I heard you got fired," Ramiro said.

"No, who told you that?"

"Someone was asking about you at a meeting, in Phoenix I think, last year, and..."

"No no, I retired; I was tired of it, especially with all the administrative baloney. I just felt there was so much more research to do, and who knows how much time one has left. What about you, Ramiro?"

"I think I'll be teaching forever. We have a meager retirement plan. But is OK, at least I still teach an insect course."

Ramiro drove through the outskirts of the city. The number of people along the streets evoked the thought of termites scurrying in the middle of a cut-open mound. What a contrast to the culture in Chinchipino, Garruty thought. All that time there, and I didn't really realize what a special place it is. His hope for mankind sank even lower.

"The virus in the U.S., it didn't get down your way?"

"The Santana Virus? No, after the epidemic broke out, they stopped all travel across the border. It appears not to have invaded Mexico."

"That's lucky," Garruty said without expression.

As they headed west toward Guadalajara, Ramiro

couldn't hold his curiosity any longer. "What's happening with you, Amos?" he asked sincerely. "Do you have serious trouble?"

"Look, my brother, I can't possibly tell you everything. I traveled back, ...um, to make a long story short, after the virus spread through the eastern United States, the authorities targeted me as a carrier, saying I was responsible for the outbreak. They were going to eliminate me, so in July I left the U.S. for Ecuador. Listen Ramiro, I met someone special. I need to get back home. Somehow I've got to cross the border without the FBI finding out."

"Amos, the epidemic has run its course. In the last two weeks, there have been very few new cases. But the death rate in a few places was nearly thirty percent."

"Thirty percent! I don't know if I'll be able to go back."

"Look Pancake, don't worry. I'm telling you, it's over. They're not looking for you anymore. Most people were immune, like you must be. You can go back anytime."

"If that's true, it's the best news I've had in months. You wouldn't believe what I've been going through."

Garruty told Ramiro about the giant walking stick he saw in Ecuador.

"Did you collect it?" asked Ramiro.

"No, it was so big, I didn't have anything to put it in!" Ramiro gave him a strange glance. "Well, actually, I couldn't stand the thought of ending the life of such a being. You wouldn't have either. You should have seen it Ramiro, it was like a different animal, more than just alive. It seemed, well, personable. Or spiritual. I can't describe it in words."

Ramiro tried to imagine the creature the way Garruty intended but admitted he wasn't sure he was able. "I guess you had to be there," he said. He'd long ago realized that Amos Garruty had a rare appreciation for insects, as if he saw something in them that no one else did.

"Yeah, even a photograph wouldn't have captured the aura of it." Garruty decided not to tell Ramiro that he heard it speak, and certainly not what it said.

"What else did you see there?" Ramiro asked.

The rest of the day, Garruty told about the many experiences he'd had in Chinchipino, especially how the people managed to exist in the jungle without destroying it. Again he stopped short of explaining their relationship with the giant walking stick, leaving Ramiro curious as to how humans could manage such a delicate balance with nature.

They spent the night in Guadalajara, and then proceeded north to Sinaloa. The remaining journey to Nogales was beset with two flat tires, a broken gas line, and a dead battery, and took four more days to complete. By the time they reached the border, the two friends, close as they were, had just about run out of things to talk about.

As they waited in the line of vehicles at the U.S. Customs gate, Ramiro asked, "Did they ever find out what happened to your mentor, Professor Quirk?"

"Not that I know of. That was the strangest thing. There was no evidence of foul play; he was in the lab that afternoon when I said good-bye to him, and then he just disappeared. That was over 30 years ago! He had the snappiest mind of anyone I ever met."

As Ramiro nudged the vehicle close to the checkpoint, Garruty turned and said, "I don't know how to thank you for taking all this time and getting me here, Ramiro."

"You don't have to say anything. Just take better care of yourself. Now tell me, where are you going from here, and how will you get there?"

"I'll rent a car and aim it east. Are you going straight back to Mexico City?"

"No, I think I'll take a few extra days and do some poking around in the mountains in Chihuahua State. There's a river there that I've wanted to explore for years. I've got a hunch there are all kinds of new insect species there — it's isolated and no one's ever collected in the area. This is the first opportunity I've ever had to stop by there."

"Ah, Chihuahua, where the weird bugs are, huh? And then a shortcut home through Durango?" Garruty chuckled.

"You're a bad man. No way, José. That's one state that won't be seeing any more of Ramiro."

"OK, my friend."

Just then the old pickup in front of them backfired. Several border guards ran toward the beat up vehicle, pointing their rifles. Several men jumped out of the back of the truck and began to run. The driver jerked the truck backwards, right into Ramiro's front bumper. Ramiro quickly backed up, and the old truck swerved and tried to turn. The driver pulled a gun and shot at the guards, who returned fire. A stray rifle bullet smashed through the side glass of the Range Rover and busted Ramiro's left carotid artery wide open. As blood gushed out, Garruty grabbed a plastic bag and pressed it over the gaping wound. He looked into Ramiro's bewildered eyes.

"What happened?"

"You've been hit. Don't talk, and don't move!"

Ramiro looked up. "I can't feel anything. You can't save me this time, Pancake. Chowwww," he whispered and slumped down behind the steering wheel.

Garruty held his fingertips to Ramiro's right carotid artery. He felt a weak pulse, then nothing. Ramiro lay in the driver's seat in a pool of blood. Garruty looked through the windshield to see the guards running across the desert, chasing the men who had fled from the pickup. Apparently no one was aware of what just happened in the Range Rover. He closed Ramiro's eyes and whispered, "So long, dear amigo, maybe I'll be seeing you soon."

Garruty grabbed his backpack and slipped out of the passenger seat of the Range Rover. He ambled to the side of the road, sat on a bench and washed the blood off his hands in a small puddle. He felt numb, as if he wasn't really there. He knew there wasn't anything he could do. After a while he somehow walked over and proceeded to go through Customs, masking his emotions about what had just happened.

In Nogales, the only rental car available immediately was a ramshackle red Escort. Garruty's overwhelming desire to hit the road persuaded him it would have to do. As he pulled out of the rental car parking lot, he argued back and forth with himself.

"It's late Pancake, you ought to get a room and wait till morning."

"Nah, you won't be able to sleep, Amos—you might as well start out tonight."

"You don't see well at night, Pancake."

"You don't see good in the daytime either, so get going."

Amos lost the argument, and headed out.

The setting sun lit the mountains ahead of him in stark contrast to the dark eastern sky. The Patagonia Highway was devoid of traffic, and in a few hours he was north of Douglas. As darkness enveloped him, he decided to take a short cut.

As he ascended the mountains, he mumbled, "It sure looks dim out there, I must have one headlight out."

He also noticed that the road was getting narrower. With one hand on the steering wheel, he pointed his penlight at the map and took another look to see if he had made a wrong turn. When he looked up he saw a sharp curve but was unable to step on the brake fast enough to make it around the sharp turn. The little car skidded and slid off the edge of the curve, stopping against a clump of small trees. Garruty gasped, relieved that the car hadn't rolled over the edge and who knows how far down the black mountainside. He gunned the accelerator, but the car was stuck.

"Damn, stranded in no man's land."

He shut the engine off and looked into the darkness. Just then the car jerked and slipped a few inches further down the steep slope. Knowing he had to get out right away, he pressed the seat belt latch. It didn't release. He pulled the door handle and pushed against the door. It wouldn't budge. The car slipped again and desperation struck his entire body. Then he heard a rapping on the window and saw someone moving his fist in a circle. Garruty rolled down the window and gasped as a hunting knife came at him. Garruty was wetting his pants when the knife cut through the seat belt in one swift motion. Then he heard a voice order, "Grab hold, if you want to survive!"

When Garruty pulled back the voice said, "Like the trapped animal that doesn't trust anyone." Suddenly the car lurched. "Grab my arms or perish!"

"Hell right!" Garruty yelled and gripped the man's arms. He got up on his haunches on the seat and the men tightened their grip on each other's arms. Garruty leaped through the window just as the small trees lost the tug of war with gravity. Together they fell backwards as the Escort plunged into the deep darkness. Garruty imagined himself tumbling down with it, bones breaking with each crunch of metal. What he felt was his rescuer loosening the grip on his arms. He did likewise.

From his knees, Garruty looked up and saw the moonlight glimmer off a bare forehead; the face, framed by long, unkempt hair, was too dimly lit to make out any features. Sitting above him on the edge of the road was a diminutive, elderly man. Garruty stuttered, "Thank you. I'd be crushed meat right now if you hadn't shown up when you did."

"Red blood, but yet the spirit beings accompany you. Forgive me; I speak the obvious. What are you doing here?"

"I was just driving through. I was in a hurry to get home, and I took my eye off the road for a second."

"Follow me, if you please."

The man led Garruty up the hill to a small dwelling hidden in the side of the mountain. Before the wreck, Garruty had noticed the lack of any sign of human habitation for miles. As they walked the rocky path, he thought, If I was going to crash, I picked the right place to get help. There's no one else living around here.

Once inside, the little man offered, "Please sit. Would you like some hot tea? You must be shaken."

Garruty could see the man was part Indian, but also with some European ancestry. He was about 5′ 6″ tall and undoubtedly in his 80s. His high forehead was wrinkled, his hair long and grayish blond; it looked like he never combed it. His skin was dark and reticulated like a dobsonfly's wings.

"Thank you, kind sir. May I ask your name?"

"You may ask, and I may answer. But first, tell me who you are."

"My name is Amos Garruty. I'm an entomologist, retired now. I (pause)…"

"…started the epidemic," the man interrupted.

Garruty gaped. "Yes, you heard no doubt; the person who wiped out America, I fear," he confessed.

"And how did you contract this virus?"

The hot tea he sipped was just the medicine he needed. He began to relax and describe his travels, trials and travails.

When it was late, the man stood, held one hand with his palm to Garruty and said, "Sleep. Tomorrow I will show you something. May your dreams be calm."

Garruty got up and bumped into the low end table situated between the two men, knocking several papers to the floor. He bent down to pick them up and caught sight of the name on one page; it read, "Prof. H. Knutts, Chiricahua Mts., AZ."

"Never mind that, you must rest now."

"Thanks. Good night," Garruty said.

Garruty didn't fall asleep right away. He was still upset about the accident and wondering how he was going to get home. But more than that, there was something familiar about the man who just rescued him. He wondered if he had seen him before.

Morning came too quickly. The smell of coffee led Garruty to the kitchen. As the two men sat having a light breakfast, they talked about the mountains and the great outdoors. They talked about a mutual interest in insects, especially that despite all the study devoted to them, there were many phenomena still unexplained.

As they finished their coffee, Garruty said, "I could swear I met you, a long time ago, but I still don't know who you are."

"All in due time. I want to show you something today. Are you ready for a short hike?"

After an hour of mostly uphill tramping, Garruty was breathing deeply and his quadriceps muscles were burning. The farther they went, the more often he had to put his hands on his knees to push himself up a steep step. He wanted to ask his leader how much longer they had to go, but he didn't want to seem weak. He was sure he wouldn't get a straight answer or any sympathy from this seemingly inhuman little being anyway.

At the top of the next ridge the man held up his left hand and stopped. "You can catch your breath now, we're close."

Garruty looked beyond the little man. In front of them, down a gradual slope, nestled in a high pocket formed by the surrounding mountains, spread a slightly hilly meadow. The unexpected array of colorful flowers in the desert mountains stunned Garruty. They slowly descended a few hundred feet until they stood on a low promontory overlooking the meadow. The number and diversity of butterflies flitting about was astounding.

The man handed Garruty his canteen. "Sit, drink, and enjoy the show."

Garruty gladly accepted the water; he sat with his legs dangling over the edge of the rock and gazed out over the meadow. The little man remained standing. He stepped to the very edge of the promontory and raised both arms above his head. He then waved his hand 27 times in pendulum-like fashion. In an instant, thousands of butterflies arose from the flowers and streamed into the sky. Garruty stood, recognizing a formation was taking place, somehow reminiscent of a marching band. Within minutes, they had formed a shimmering aerial image of a butterfly.

"Sky ballet," whispered Garruty, stupefied.

A few seconds after the huge butterfly image was complete, the man lowered his arms and the butterflies descended to the flowers. The little man turned toward Garruty. "Did you see other than with your eyes?" he asked.

"I saw something miraculous; something I would not have imagined," Garruty replied.

"There is more you will see."

After the butterflies had sipped nectar for a few minutes, the little man stood and raised his arms again. This time he waved his hand five times, upon which green, blue and black butterflies ascended, and high in the sky, formed the image of a dragonfly. Garruty giggled with glee. Again the man dropped his arms and the butterflies returned to the flowers. After that, the man used a different wave to signal the butterflies to form a different image every 15 minutes. By late afternoon, all 28 of the insect orders had been configured.

Garruty sat there awe-struck; he finally asked, "How did you find this place?"

"I don't know. I mean, I don't remember how I got here. The first fifty-some years of my life have been erased. I met two men of Apache descent, and they helped me settle here. They named me Professor Knutts, undoubtedly because I was always philosophizing."

"Did they give you a first name?"

"They didn't have to. For some reason, that was the only thing that came back to me, my given first name, Herod."

Garruty started adding things up. He knew only one person named Herod, and that was his mentor, Dr. Herod

Quirk. Could this be him? He's the right height, and he would be his age.

Garruty studied his mysterious companion for a moment, seeing what he thought were some familiar facial features, but then caught himself. If he's really the long-lost Quirk, did he suffer amnesia and wander into the desert southwest somehow? Would it be dangerous to tell him who he is, or rather, who he was? I can't be sure it's him, and besides, what good would it do? He's happy here.

Prof. Knutts broke his chain of thought. "Well, show's over and it's late. We better go back."

The trek back to the dwelling was much easier. It was nearly dark when they got there. The Professor handed Garruty an odd-shaped glass filled with a clear, pleasingly aromatic liquid.

"A local liqueur, for the tongue."

They lifted their glasses and sipped. After a long silence, Professor Knutts spoke. "I have a friend who usually comes by here in the morning. You might catch a ride with him to Portal."

"I hope so. I'm indebted to you already. Just that I'm—

"—anxious to get home. You'll find what you seek."

Garruty felt there was more to his words than what was at the surface. He said good night, realizing that it was time to leave. I've got to recover that hand lens, he thought.

It was mid-morning when Jim Strongbow stopped at Prof. Knutt's hillside and agreed to give Garruty a ride. The bright sun was blinding and Garruty had lost his sunglasses. The big Native American said little during the trip. It took a long two hours to get to the small town of Portal.

To Garruty's dismay, there was no car rental place and no bus station. Fortunately he had enough cash to buy a 1973 Chevy pickup that Strongbow told him was for sale. By afternoon, he was heading east again. He decided to do his best to concentrate on nothing but his driving and the scenery. Despite his conviction to limit his thoughts, there was one thought he couldn't prevent: he knew that he would automatically smile whenever he saw a butterfly flutter by. Garruty saw very few people as he drove through the western countryside. Well, that's not unusual out here. Folks are widely scattered. He stopped outside of Dallas and tried to call Carmela, but he got no answer.

Four days later, in the late afternoon, the pickup hobbled and smoked through Memphis, Tennessee. He tried Carmela's number again to no avail. He drove to Big Hill Pond State Park and camped out that night, relishing the fall weather. Early the next morning, he drove the short distance to Clifton. About a mile before he got there, at a narrow bridge on a back road, the old pickup belched its last stroke. Garruty gave it its last rites and waited for awhile, but no one came by. He thought, All the creeks around here flow to the Tennessee River. He remembered seeing a map of the area and was pretty sure this was Buckeye Branch, the mouth of which was a short distance upstream from his favorite big rock.

"If I wade down it, it might be a shortcut. I hope these old running shoes hold up," he muttered as he splashed in.

10

Delirium Insectorum

Stumbling over stones, with tightly packed sand in the tips of his old running shoes cramming his toes and little trickles of sweat stinging his tired eyes, Garruty needed a break. He set his backpack on a large rock and planted his behind down in the cool, shallow riffle. Though he had seen Buckeye Branch on a map before, he was unfamiliar with it. After wading down its meandering course for an hour, he felt he was getting close to his destination, the Tennessee River, but he didn't know if he had enough strength left to get there. October was one of his favorite months, as it brought a respite from hot humid weather, but you could have squeezed water out of the air on this day. As he bathed his bottom, he slowly garnered strength. A slight breeze loosed a small covey of orange-brown leaves and they showered down around him. The dry, slightly curled cadavers cascaded, twirling and zigzagging, finally nestling onto the flowing water and casting out on their foreordained journey. He looked up and gazed at the hazy blue sky through the thinning canopy. He breathed in deeply.

"OK, Pancake, you can do this," he encouraged himself.

He washed the uninvited grit out of his shoes, then soaked his sweatband in the clear water and put it back over his forehead. He straightened his creaky knees and started downstream again.

The edges of the small stream were tangled with brush, briars and poison ivy. It was difficult enough navigating over the stones and fallen branches in the creek bed, but the thought of trying a short cut over land made him feel even more exasperated. The painful memory of the poison ivy in New Jersey fortified his decision to stay with the winding, watery corridor. As he rounded a bend in the stream, he saw an opening along the right bank. At one point, the edge was mowed, as recently as a couple of weeks ago. Garruty decided to slip quietly past the property, hoping no one was watching. When he got to the mowed area, he looked uphill and saw a small cabin a few hundred feet away; it looked abandoned. Then he spotted a small canoe lying upside down, one end in the water, at the corner of the kept property.

Hmmm, if I had that to float in, bet I could make it to the big river for sure. Looks like there's nobody around to ask permission. I'll only be borrowing it, thinking how he could rationalize his thievery.

Garruty looked around and then carefully turned the canoe right side up. A medium-sized copperhead, about two feet long and vividly marked, quickly vacated its hiding place and slithered underneath the closest dead leaves.

"You better not be here when those hunters get back," he whispered to the little serpent.

Garruty glanced up at the cabin once more, then grabbed the paddle and eased the canoe into the water. He tossed his backpack in, carefully stepped into the canoe and sat on the narrow seat at the tail end. The metal bottom scraped a few stones at first, but soon he was off and floating downstream. It felt good to be moving with so little effort. All he had to do was steer to miss rocks and shallow spots, although occasionally he had to pull the canoe through extremely shallow riffles and around fallen branches. After floating for about a half mile, the stream became a little deeper; it looked as if there was a break in the tree canopy ahead. I must be getting pretty close to the big river, he thought and put the paddle across his lap.

Even though he hadn't had to row or steer the canoe much, the weakness in his arms was plainly evident; biceps cramps weren't far off. He knew his physical condition was poor and he was pretty sure he would have some sore muscles for the next few days. The almost constant hardships since the spring had taken quite a toll on him. He had lost at least 20 pounds, and he hadn't been able to follow his usual walking-jogging regimen. The conditioning he had maintained most of his adult life had gotten him through the past five onerous months, but now his stamina was at an all-time low. He was thankful that the water had gotten deep enough so he wouldn't have to expend as much energy maneuvering the canoe.

As he drifted downstream, carried by the water's power, he tried to relax his mind and body. Concentrating on the natural beauty of a stream had always buoyed him up. He fixated on the clear, flowing water and the orange and tan gravel over which darters darted. He imagined seeing the little fishes in their spring spawning reds, greens, yellows and blues. How precarious an existence, to be so dependent on undisturbed habitat, so close to annihilation, he thought.

Soon his mind turned back to the present. Near-death experiences. I've had enough myself this summer to fill a lifetime. Regrets, same-same, he thought. He thought about home.

"Tinker! God I miss her, I hope she's all right." He felt a strong desire to make sure. He then thought about Carmela. Was she dead? he wondered.

He thought about going back to Atlanta to find out if she had survived. What am I going to do? He plucked the flower head off a white aster stretching from the bank out over the water. Each time he pulled off a petal, he said either 'Alabama' or 'Atlanta'. With just a few petals left, the thought occurred to him, maybe it doesn't have to be either-or. What if...

But before he could finish that thought, a strange sound caught his attention. What sounded like a breeze swooshing through the leaves had interrupted his decision making, but when he looked up he could see no movement.

Not a single leaf had fallen, and not one was even quivering. He looked down and noticed that the water had become still, and his canoe was oddly motionless. He lowered the paddle and stroked it through the water; nothing moved, not even a swirl at the water's surface. It was as if time had been suspended. There was no sound, no movement whatsoever.

At first Garruty looked all around, then he crouched and moved to the middle seat of the canoe, straddling it and staring at the bank for any minute movement. Total stillness. He closed his eyes and listened intently. Total quiet. He felt the hair on his arms and the back of his neck stand up and then he had a strong premonition that something was about to happen.

For some incomprehensible reason, Garruty couldn't open his eyes. He sat there, beginning to think that he also was frozen in time. The next thing he noticed was a slight rustling sound and then a bedlam of clicking and thumping sounds, like hollow bones hitting metal. All of a sudden he felt something claw-like cling to his left arm and something finger-like quiver against his right temple. Reluctantly he opened his eyes and slowly peered from one side to the other; he was appalled at what he saw. Perched on the end seats of the canoe were two huge, translucent insect forms surrounded by a swirling, misty fog. On his left was an enormous long-winged, grayish-blue insect that Garruty recognized as a primitive dragonfly. Its two pale reddish eyes were widely separated and its heavy, toothed mandibles protruded. It had two pairs of long, straight-veined wings on the bulky part of its limestone gray thorax. Garruty also saw a pair of winglets on the first segment of its thorax. It was stockier than modern-day dragonflies. The ominous figure was touching Garruty's left arm with the claws of its front legs.

On his right was a form unfamiliar to Garruty. It had three pairs of rather short wing-like extensions on its thorax. These "flaps" did not appear completely hinged at their bases, indicating they were for gliding. Garruty suspected it represented an early stage in the evolution of truly functional wings, which would have made it much more ancient than the pre-dragonfly on his left. The ghost's body was pale greenish-gray. It had simple chewing mouthparts and long pectinate antennae. The prickly bumps on top of its head and the gray, sunken-in eyes completed its vivid appearance. He detected a pungent odor, somewhat like the musky smell cockroaches emit. Ghosts of Insects Past, he thought.

Uncomfortable as he was at the touch of these monstrous insect forms, Garruty didn't move. In fact, except for trembling, he felt immobilized. The more ancient ghost on his right pressed its lobed antennae against his temples. Suddenly he realized he was beginning to receive mental images, a "slide show" of diverse, ancient insect groups. As the images crawled, hopped, glided and flapped through a time window in his mind, he could hear their shrill, almost mournful sounds. He began to see how insects diverged early in the Paleozoic era, different groups arising and then becoming extinct. He saw whole groups of strange forms improve flight capabilities. Many "experimental" wing types died out after millions of years and then re-emerged. Clearly, winged insect lineages were more complex and much richer than any paleontologist had ever proposed.

Next he saw how insects had coevolved with almost every kind of plant and animal group. Herbivorous forms were being showcased, especially how they evolved ways to attack all types of plant defenses, and also how they evolved means to escape predation. The antennae pressed tighter against his temples. Slowly the ancient visions began to fade and gradate into linguistic messages.

At first the signal was unclear, but soon Garruty began to comprehend: "Basic insect design. Instinct." Then a pause. "Successful life forms." There was a longer pause. "Human species treats all life with conquering, dismissal." The voice became more coherent. "Until humans respect and appreciate all other living things, they do not live in harmony with nature. This disregard creates great suffering and loss. Humans are derived from the earth; once they obeyed its natural laws—they will again, this is inevitable."

Garruty noticed the antennae slipping from his temples; at the same time the claws of the giant dragonfly dug deeper into his left arm. He turned toward his other ghostly visitor. He looked down to see blood oozing from the punctures, but he did not feel pain. He turned and looked into the ghost's bulging pale-red compound eyes, trying to resist its stare but unable to do so. Compelled by a riveting force, and not knowing which lens facet to look into, he stared into the middle of its eyes.

The ghost whirred it wings and rose slightly without loosening its grip on his arm; it moved closer to Garruty until it was only about a foot from his face and then perched. Although Garruty could not hear definite words, he sensed that the ghost was somehow communicating thoughts. Its first message came to him in a low, hollow, resonant and vibrating tone; he managed to translate, "I lived...what you call...Upper Carboniferous Period." This was the time that Garruty yearned to learn about most in his life.

"Why do you haunt me, ancient odonatoid?" Garruty asked the ghastly figure.

The ghost shook and then communicated, "You not understand... <u>You</u> seek ancient past... <u>You</u> called <u>us</u> here."

Garruty started to ask, "Did modern dragonflies stem from..." but the ghost dug its claws deeper into his arm, shook itself again, and ordered, "You must listen now. All your life you investigate insects, asking how they live and why they do what they do."

"That's true, I..." Garruty conveyed back.

"Do not interrupt now!" the ghost bellowed. It lowered itself slightly and then resumed sending its message. "You cannot understand insects. Your kind is unlike any other species in the history of life on earth. Your species needs to control—you do not accept what you do not like. Instead you try to change everything around you. All other species accept what they cannot control."

Garruty saw a hologram depicting a chipmunk being captured by a cat, and after an initial resistance, how it accepted its fate. He saw that humans could not accept such a fate; in fact most of them could not even accept the cat's act of killing. He realized he was seeing the perspective of a predatory existence originating from the beginning of life. "Who are humans to question or challenge the relationships among living things?" the apparition fired into Garruty's brain, but this was not posed as a question.

The ghost released its death-like grip, but then immediately repositioned its claws further up his arm. The messages continued. "Humans claim ownership, whereas no other living things on earth own anything; owning, even one's life, is a non-phenomenon."

The ghost further conveyed to Garruty that by controlling their environment, the human species escaped universal laws such as natural selection and population dynamics, but only temporarily. It added that this could not go on without consequences. This last message was faint, and Garruty sensed that the apparition was shuddering, its touch becoming lighter, as if it were weakening. He started to convey his greatest respect and appreciation to this foreboding entity.

Total silence suddenly entered Garruty's mind, and he caught a glimpse of a massive insect extinction. He then felt both clammy visitors begin to withdraw from contact. He tried to convey his gratitude for the insight he gained, but they reacted as if they did not understand this concept.

He then pleaded for an answer to a notion that had intrigued him for years, "Are all insects of earthly origin?"

He detected an image of sarcastic, misanthropic smiles; then he heard a faint rustling as the ghosts lifted upward. They slowly faded and vanished in the rising fog.

Garruty was so shaken he forgot where he was and what he was doing. He even wondered if he was actually still alive. With a shake of his head, he tried to come to his senses. Did that happen? he wondered. He pressed his fingertips to his temples and felt several elongate, parallel indentations in his skin. He looked at his left arm and saw four small holes surrounded by dark red, dry blood. Oh, boy; oh, real, he concluded. The vivid images and chilling messages dominated his thoughts for several minutes. He trembled for at least half an hour.

Garruty took a deep breath and looked around. The forest was eerily quiet. He pushed the end of the paddle against the stream bottom, but the canoe didn't budge. He decided to get out of the canoe, but just then the sky flashed in blinding pulses as if a huge strobe light suddenly had been turned on. He heard a high-pitched whine. Oh man, what now? No, I don't wanna see, he thought and squeezed his eyelids down tight.

The next thing he heard was a clamor of claws scratching against the metal bottom of the canoe. Then he felt those claws clinging to his legs. His eyes opened involuntarily and he saw two very different insect forms. He was thankful that they weren't as large as the ones that had just terrified him. Crawling up his left leg was an iridescent tan beetle. It was about 10" long and had short pink antennae. Its wing covers were scoop-shaped and when held together formed an elongate bowl with twelve trails curving up to the edges. At the bottom of this bowl were twelve wiggling, grayish brown larvae.

Crawling up his right leg was an insect unlike anything Garruty had ever seen or imagined. It was vaguely similar to a bumblebee, with blue and white hairs in concentric circles around its chunky body. It was also 10" long but with very long white antennae. Garruty noticed that its four short, wide wings were not made of normal insect cuticle, and instead of a stinger there was a long narrow tube on the end of its flexible abdomen. The strange insects were translucent as were the Ghosts of Insects Past. They slowly crawled up and over his knees and perched on his horizontal thighs. Garruty sat as still as he possibly could. The insects touched their antennae to his skin and he began to receive a euphonic message emanating from both apparitions.

"We are 'Insects Yet to Come.' We appear to you from a future time when insects evolve intelligence to augment their instinctive powers."

The apparitions previewed a future in which insects once again would dominate the earth, especially after a long period of mass extinction. He saw some species, representing new major groups, evolving genes that utilized discarded synthetic materials in the building of tissues. The ghosts then communicated separately.

"As you see before you, I, the Flechette Waspdred, have plastic in my wings." The waspdred then demonstrated the tube at the end of its abdomen. It aimed at Garruty's backpack and quickly fired three small darts into the small trademark tab. "The darts are tipped with a toxin that stops my prey in its tracks." The mushroom beetle then showed Garruty how it could crawl beneath the cap of a mature mushroom to feed its larvae; the larvae found safety in the hollow of their mother's wing covers.

The apparitions shifted their antennae and continued. The next scene revealed to Garruty involved mankind. He saw that in the future, man would continue to develop technology at an ever-increasing pace.

"Mankind could change the earth in ways that would bring doom to themselves. Going backward in time presents dangers, like transporting extinct viruses, microbes transmitted by extinct insects that humans cannot fight off. There were microorganisms that infected early primates, decimating populations and causing extinctions. Man would be extremely susceptible to these rapidly changing germs."

The speed of the messages then slowed. "Human beings have two abilities that insects do not possess. They can see beauty and they can feel love; these are vital forces for humans and keys to their salvation, yet few individuals know them fully. The irony is that people who do not maximize these gifts will not complete their sought-after spiritual journey." The signal after this last message faded out and the apparitions became silent.

Garruty felt the insects loosen their grip on his thighs and start to lift into the air. As they were leaving, he frantically begged, "Are there Ghosts of Insects Present?"

The apparitions turned back and deflected their antennae to touch him again, "You imply they are not with you."

Garruty pleaded, "Why me!?"

"Many are bitten, but so few smitten," came their last message. In a split second they vanished.

Garruty felt suddenly chilly. Again the air was still and the canoe was motionless as if aground. But before he could get out of the canoe, a dead branch fell from a hackberry tree and crashed loudly to the ground. A male mockingbird warbled away, practicing the many different birds' songs he learned to mimic. Garruty pinched his leg—he was alive. He quickly checked the water. It was flowing again, and he felt the canoe start to move with the current. The paddle quickly struck with such renewed vigor that water splashed up in Garruty's face, which served to break his solemn mood.

Things seemed normal enough, but Garruty was worried. Ghosts from the Past, Apparitions from the Future, I don't know. That leaves out the present; what about Insect Spirits of the Present?

He looked and listened. Are they coming to haunt me next? Garruty kept paddling, as the water had gotten deeper and slowed. A short distance ahead, he saw a large opening in the tree canopy; he was anxious to get away from what he regarded as the "Stream of Insect Ghosts".

Garruty scanned the big river as he slowly guided the canoe into the powerful current. The air over the river was lighter and moving at a brisker pace than in the protected tributary, helping push him downriver. He stayed near the bank. There wasn't another boat within sight; there wasn't even an outboard motor within earshot.

In less than an hour, Garruty pulled up to the boat ramp upstream of Clifton and slid the canoe up on the sandy edge. Slinging his backpack over his shoulder, he walked up to the big rock he had sat on over four months before. His anxiety as to whether his hand lens and vial were still where he had forgotten them was quickly answered. He pulled the two precious items from deep in the crack and slipped them inside his pocket, mumbling, "Thank goodness!"

Garruty sat down and leaned up against the rock. He took off his wet shoes and socks and wiggled his toes. He recorded the recent events in his journal, trying to keep from reliving too vividly the ghostly visitations. Then he closed his eyes and listened. He expected total silence and anticipated more spirits, the Insect Spirits of the Present, to come clambering all over him.

"I might as well wait here for'em," he resigned himself.

The first image he thought about was a katydid; he imagined its long antennae tickling his leg to no end. Uneventful minutes passed. Just as Garruty was about to doze off, he felt something tickle his left heel. He quickly jerked his leg away and looked down at his foot. Scurrying away was a beetle. Garruty scanned the river, the air, the trees; all seemed normal. Besides, the previous ghosts didn't flee from him; they sought him and stayed. This beetle was opaque and less than an inch long; it looked real enough. He quickly reached down and picked up the struggling beetle from the loose sand. It was a rove beetle, dull brown and orange, a kind he had never seen before.

"Hello little friend. Let's see, I bet your name is Squelchy. You're real, aren't you? You wouldn't believe what I've been seeing. Or maybe you would."

Garruty held me gently in his fingers and spoke to me as if I were a colleague of his. The whole rest of the day, he described his experiences and trials, starting with his time travel in May. He spoke as if it was all happening again.

When he finished, he set me down on his backpack and said, "Make whatever use of my journals you want, Squelchy. All the torturous details I might not have told you about are in there. I don't think I'll need them anymore. I'll hang onto these though." He tucked his old field notebooks under his left arm.

He seemed relieved, like a beaten boxer who had finally laid his gloves down. At that he ambled down to the canoe, slipped it in the water and pushed off, turning down river. He spoke aloud as he drifted.

"What did they mean, that I assumed they're not with me? I see them all the time; I just talked to one for hours. Did I imagine that? Wait a minute, is that what the Apparitions from the Future meant? I've been imagining Insects Present and didn't know it!? Now that I think about all the strange happenings since going back in time and seeing dragonflies doctoring snakes—like the ants taking me to court, the underwater fireflies, and on and on all summer. Could it be my imagination ran wild and became my reality—like was I utterly bugged? It seemed there would be no end to it. Could there be peace of mind ahead for me?"

As he floated away, with paddle across his knees and the sinking sun searing the clouds smeared across the western sky, a sweet, soft voice wafted up from the singing river. I sensed comfort in his demeanor when the lines from that bluegrass, spiritualistic song, "Lone Pilgrim," emanated from the surging current:

"And gathering storms may arise
But calm is my feeling
At rest is my soul
The tears are all wiped from my eyes."

I don't know how much, if anything, of what he told me actually happened. I surely don't know what happened to him after he disappeared around the bend of the river. I have to put this all behind me now, as these shortening day lengths mean my time is creeping away.

THE END

About the author

Utterly Bugged is Ken Tennessen's first novella. He writes poetry and short stories, as well as technical articles on insects. He calls Wisconsin home but travels widely, mostly researching and photographing dragonflies.

About the artist

Kika Esteves is a Brazilian illustrator and comic artist. She was born in 1979 and graduated with a degree in Marketing and Advertisement Studies. She lives in Natal - Brazil with her husband and 2 yellow cats.